MORTIMER TRIPPE AT SEA

David Hancock

en Press

First published in Great Britain by Pen Press

All paper used in the printing of this book has been made from wood grown in managed, sustainable forests.

ISBN13: 978-1-78003-166-8

Printed and bound in the UK
Pen Press is an imprint of
Indepenpress Publishing Limited
25 Eastern Place
Brighton
BN2 1GJ

Cover design by Jacqueline Abromeit

Born in Sheffield on 16 April 1939, David Hancock lived his early life with his parents and identical twin brother in Hathersage in Derbyshire. He attended St Anselm's Preparatory School, and later Oundle, before going to St John's College, Oxford, where he read French and German for two terms, then Politics, Philosophy and Economics. He was called to the Bar by Lincoln's Inn in 1965, but later left practice as a Barrister to work as a legal adviser in industry, travelling world-wide. Married and living in London, his hobby was writing. On retirement he was able to pursue his writing on a full time basis until his death on 21 February 2009 following an illness. This is his third book of the Mortimer Trippe trilogy.

To Moura
With Love
from Jacqui

To Jacquie

CHAPTER 1

The island of Malou has for long been known by the small band of enthusiasts who visit it, to be the most delightfully eccentric and mysterious of the Channel Islands, although the local residents take a less sanguine view of its charms. Furthermore, Malou has recently attained some notoriety as the scene of what, had it succeeded, would have been among the most heinous art crimes of all time. The frustration of this outrage was due to the vigilance and acuity of a man who was to all appearances an employee of the Castle Hotel, the sole hotel of note on the Island: Mr Mortimer Trippe, of the Four Eyes Private Enquiry Agency.

Anyone who finds the island of Malou strange has probably not visited its little Hebridean sister Radichsay, or not penetrated beyond the small but elegant White Lady Hotel. Radichsay's principal ornament, which stands at the head of its own white beach and has its own separate jetty, no doubt so that its well-heeled guests should not be sullied by contact with the odd people and odder goings-on, of what little else there is of this sequestered isle.

Radichsay has few inhabitants and those that there are are reticent and surly to an extent not usually found even in the Western Isles. They are mostly either crofters or employees (fewer than a dozen in number) of the Radichsay distillery. These latter are reputed to consume a great deal of their own product, although this is never translated into any discernible conviviality, or even civility. The man who seems to take the keenest pleasure in Radichsay whisky is the owner of the distillery, as indeed he is the owner of all else on the Island, even though the White Lady Hotel is subject to a long lease. This landowner is no other than the Thane, Malcolm MacRadich, 24th Captain of Clanradich, whose clan, numbering fewer than a hundred souls, is the smallest as well as the most obscure in Scotland. The Laird resides in a state of celibacy (but only in the strict sense of remaining unmarried) in Fort Radich, an ancient granite structure, which overlooks his domain from the crest of Ben Radich, a modest eminence of four hundred feet at most.

The most frequent visitors to the Chieftain's lair have for some time been the nuns from the Radichsay Nunnery. These ladies are, according to rumour, young, good-looking and blonde, and swim regularly, unclothed, in the chill brine of the vast ocean, warmed as it is here by the soothing waters of the North Atlantic Drift. In the manner of the Loch Ness monster, if so odious a comparison with such divine creatures may be made, the sightings of this phenomenon are said to be rare and unconfirmed. In summer and on the more clement evenings of winter the nuns, wearing their fetching white habits, each adorned with a single large cross of canary-yellow, progress up the hill from the Nunnery to the Laird's fort, whence then emanate strange sounds, said to be of merriment and even of most unnunnish dissipation. The returning white crocodile, however, is every bit as decorous as had been the dignified procession up the hill before the sisters had attended whatever revel might have taken place.

The Laird himself is reputedly a very rough diamond indeed and 'a thoroughly bad lot': not only barely literate but cruel, despotic and dissolute. This ogre lives virtually alone in his unheated and crumbling fortress, with just two Gaelic-only speaking menservants for company, both MacRadich clansmen. Doubtless through interbreeding, one is stone-deaf, while the other, built like an Olympic shot-putter, is a monosyllabic halfwit.

The White Lady Hotel is not merely given over to pleasure but is dedicated to the style and customs of an earlier age. Built in and typical of the Edwardian era, it had its hey-day between the two World Wars, but this has been consciously prolonged by a continuing insistence on the part of successive proprietors of the hotel. The values and mores, including dress, of the inter-war period should be maintained; smoking, for example, while not obligatory, is encouraged, the recent governmental ban being universally ignored owing to the lack of anyone to enforce it. The main rooms are not only decorated in the art deco manner beloved particularly of the more progressive visitors of the twenties and thirties, but contain a profusion of Edwardiana dating from the reign before the world changed forever. The Prince of Wales, was later to patronize the White Lady before it was so named, in the company of his mistress Mrs Keppel, the *beau monde* of the time inevitably following in their wake. Later, accompanied by the future Duchess of Windsor, the hedonistic Prince again visited what was then still called the Radichsay Hotel on several occasions. He always occupied the vast bedroom at the front with the most extensive view of the sea. The room has, since her death, been reputed to have been haunted by the ghost of Mrs Simpson, seated on the four-poster bed in white evening gown and picking at a lobster. This apparition is almost certainly the inspiration for the relatively recent change of name of the hotel.

Upon this Hebridean idyll, in the late morning of a cloudless summer's day, there landed Mr Mortimer Trippe, private detective. Mortimer was here at the behest of a new client, who had telephoned him at home, quite out of the blue, and introduced herself as Lady Bertha Hook. Her ladyship had informed the sleuth that she was dispatching him on a mission of vengeance in order to atone for a great wrong which had been done to her. At this stage he was merely to watch and listen to those against whom she was seeking retribution, a group of four women and one man – if such he could be called – who would shortly also be arriving on the island. More would be explained when the occasion was opportune.

* * *

The Castle Hotel on Malou is so named because it forms part of the ancient Norman castle of Malou, which stands sentinel over the small and disorderly capital town of St Luke, and which has been the seat of the Seigneurs of Malou since the tenth century. It was from behind the screen of his temporary position as a waiter and general factotum in this unsuspecting establishment, that Mortimer Trippe had carried out the investigation which led to the downfall of the plotters of the fiendish scheme which had amounted to no less than an attempt to steal the almost priceless de Lessay collection of paintings.

In the hotel now, apparently on their summer holiday, two ladies were staying; that is to say, they were supposed by staff and fellow-guests alike to be ladies. The older and stouter of these two, Lady Bertha Hook by name, shared some of the characteristics of the Island: she was probably, amid considerable competition, one of the most eccentric of the higher ranks of the English aristocracy and had about her a faintly perceptible aura of both mystery and criminality. Large and coarse-featured, she did not pretend to good looks, and was delicate in neither appearance nor manner; her companion was a young woman of a quite different stamp: leaving aside some bastardy a generation or two back, this filly was said to be entirely English, although she had the shining eyes and skin of the South Seas and her flowing raven locks looked naked without the garlands of exotic flowers which should rightly have adorned them. The two were now seated at dinner in the hotel dining-room, recognizably a former Norman chapel and still containing stained glass

CHAPTER 2

The five-strong party from London had just braved a sea-journey from Colonsay, a small island of the Inner Hebrides – although a good deal larger that Radichsay – in a thirty-foot open boat. The weather for the crossing had been calm and the sea, most unusually, like glass. Having breakfasted early, the travellers were pleasantly animated by the prospect of luncheon at the White Lady Hotel and keenly anticipated the liquid refreshment which would both precede and accompany it. Chrysalis-like, they were ready to shed their outer casing of hats and cloaks and to emerge as butterflies, ready for all that awaited them. At the hotel's private jetty the new arrivals were assisted ashore by two boatmen wearing the white and green livery of the hotel, and were then helped out of their outer garments before entering the white and green painted conservatory which protrudes over a significant portion of the dazzling white beach. Here, the emergent butterflies were greeted obsequiously by Mr Humphrey Bliss – manager and maître d'hôtel. He invited his new guests to be seated at one of the low tables where drinks were taken and from which they would be able to study in detail both the cocktail and wine lists and the luncheon menu. Humphrey Bliss had floppy fair hair, through which he constantly ran a hand, a slender nose and chin, and the petulant mouth of a spoilt six-year old.

The newly arrived travellers would have been horrified had they known that they in turn were the objects of a scrutiny just as keen as their own lists of food and drink on offer. For in

windows and other anachronistic artefacts more associated with worship than with the pleasures of the table. The world at large might well have gained the impression that the younger woman was somehow subservient to the older, but this was probably because Cissie Sykes spoke so little; when she did, however, it was in the distinctive and on occasion haughty tones of the traditional English upper class, unaffected by modern idiom or inflexion.

"So what did you tell this Trippe chap, Bertha?"

"Not a lot. It was on the phone. But enough to induce him to go up there."

Cissie laughed. "So he knows about the Sisterhood, as you call them?"

"Only in very general terms."

"Including the fact that you used to be one of them and that they're –"

Bertha held up a hand and glanced round the nearly full dining-room. "Careful what you say, Cis," she said in a low voice. "Anyway, no. But he'll work it out soon enough, if he's half as smart as I think he is."

Lady Bertha naturally knew of the recent history of Malou and had been much interested in the infamous conduct which had so nearly come to fruition there; particularly in the manner of its prevention, virtually unaided, by a London private detective. (Knowing that it would impede his future investigative work, if his name became at all well known, Mr Lamplighter, the sole proprietor of the Four Eyes Agency, had sensibly managed to keep Mortimer personally almost entirely free of publicity, but had been far from reticent in allowing fame and glory to be heaped upon the Agency itself.) Her ladyship had come to this, until lately, obscure Channel Island – accompanied as so often by young Cissie Sykes – in the hope of finding the private eye still here. Being informed that he had recently returned to London, she had obtained his telephone number from the hotel maid Barbara and had been surprised when it had turned out to be the detective's private, and not his professional, number. She had already found out from the supposedly confidential secretary of the Sisterhood, whom Bertha still prudently kept 'sweet', that her erstwhile colleagues would be plotting their next outrage from the peaceful little Hebridean island of Radichsay, and it was accordingly thither that she had dispatched her private eye.

"God, the food in this place is foul," announced Cissie, stabbing a piece of putrescent fish which a sullen waiter had placed in front of her.

Lady Bertha summoned the waiter with an imperious click of her muscular fingers.

"What is this repulsive object supposed to be, waiter?"

"It's the main course, my lady."

"The main course? I have no recollection of having a first course. What became of it?"

The 'soup of the day' had in fact run out shortly before Lady Bertha and her companion had come belatedly down for dinner.

"Well, it –"

"Don't prevaricate, waiter. Either you forgot to serve it or it ran out. One or the other. Which?"

"It ran out, my lady."

"I see. And this … main course, you call it? What is it supposed to be?"

"Halibut, I believe, my lady."

"Rubbish," snorted Lady Bertha ambiguously. "But whatever it is, it is clearly inedible."

"Everyone else has eaten it."

"That is of no consequence. I require you to remove it at once. Bring me a beefsteak and fried potato-chips instead. The meat to be bloody."

The waiter, a very strict vegetarian, shuddered. "We don't have any steak and chips. There is nothing else but the fish, my lady."

"And what is the Seigneur dining on, might I ask? Not this filth, I'll wager." Lady Bertha knew that the Seigneur's

quarters in the Castle shared a kitchen, though not with the hotel.

"Well –" the waiter was reluctant to say what the Seigneur was having – indeed almost invariably had – for dinner.

"Speak up, man." Looking round the dining-room, Lady Bertha saw faces turned towards her, uniformly irritated and impatient. "Come, waiter. Don't be shy."

The waiter looked round the room and took a deep breath. "Tonight," he said, for all to hear, "the Seigneur is dining on frogs' legs and haggis."

A stunned silence was quickly followed by gales of derisive laughter.

"Excellent," said Lady Bertha with apparent relish. "Then that is what I too shall have."

"Very good, my lady." With an inward smirk, the obedient servant took away the unwanted fish and withdrew to fetch Lady Bertha's order.

"Serve you bloody right, Bert," hissed Cissie, who had now decided to rely on bread and wine for sustenance. "Teach you a fucking lesson."

"Cheeky, stuck-up little bitch," snarled her ladyship, aka Bert Pyman, under his breath, and in a pronounced London accent which never failed to make Cissie cringe. "I'll teach *you* a lesson all right when we get upstairs, you see if I don't."

windows and other anachronistic artefacts more associated with worship than with the pleasures of the table. The world at large might well have gained the impression that the younger woman was somehow subservient to the older, but this was probably because Cissie Sykes spoke so little; when she did, however, it was in the distinctive and on occasion haughty tones of the traditional English upper class, unaffected by modern idiom or inflexion.

"So what did you tell this Trippe chap, Bertha?"

"Not a lot. It was on the phone. But enough to induce him to go up there."

Cissie laughed. "So he knows about the Sisterhood, as you call them?"

"Only in very general terms."

"Including the fact that you used to be one of them and that they're –"

Bertha held up a hand and glanced round the nearly full dining-room. "Careful what you say, Cis," she said in a low voice. "Anyway, no. But he'll work it out soon enough, if he's half as smart as I think he is."

Lady Bertha naturally knew of the recent history of Malou and had been much interested in the infamous conduct which had so nearly come to fruition there; particularly in the manner of its prevention, virtually unaided, by a London private detective. (Knowing that it would impede his future investigative work, if his name became at all well known, Mr Lamplighter, the sole proprietor of the Four Eyes Agency, had sensibly managed to keep Mortimer personally almost entirely free of publicity, but had been far from reticent in allowing fame and glory to be heaped upon the Agency itself.) Her ladyship had come to this, until lately, obscure Channel Island – accompanied as so often by young Cissie Sykes – in the hope of finding the private eye still here. Being informed that he had recently returned to London, she had obtained his telephone number from the hotel maid Barbara and had been surprised when it had turned out to be the detective's private, and not his professional, number. She had already found out from the supposedly confidential secretary of the Sisterhood, whom Bertha still prudently kept 'sweet', that her erstwhile colleagues would be plotting their next outrage from the peaceful little Hebridean island of Radichsay, and it was accordingly thither that she had dispatched her private eye.

"God, the food in this place is foul," announced Cissie, stabbing a piece of putrescent fish which a sullen waiter had placed in front of her.

Lady Bertha summoned the waiter with an imperious click of her muscular fingers.

"What is this repulsive object supposed to be, waiter?"

"It's the main course, my lady."

"The main course? I have no recollection of having a first course. What became of it?"

The 'soup of the day' had in fact run out shortly before Lady Bertha and her companion had come belatedly down for dinner.

"Well, it –"

"Don't prevaricate, waiter. Either you forgot to serve it or it ran out. One or the other. Which?"

"It ran out, my lady."

"I see. And this … main course, you call it? What is it supposed to be?"

"Halibut, I believe, my lady."

"Rubbish," snorted Lady Bertha ambiguously. "But whatever it is, it is clearly inedible."

"Everyone else has eaten it."

"That is of no consequence. I require you to remove it at once. Bring me a beefsteak and fried potato-chips instead. The meat to be bloody."

The waiter, a very strict vegetarian, shuddered. "We don't have any steak and chips. There is nothing else but the fish, my lady."

"And what is the Seigneur dining on, might I ask? Not this filth, I'll wager." Lady Bertha knew that the Seigneur's quarters in the Castle shared a kitchen, though not a chef, with the hotel.

"Well –" the waiter was reluctant to say what the Seigneur was having – indeed almost invariably had – for dinner.

"Speak up, man." Looking round the dining-room, Lady Bertha saw faces turned towards her, uniformly irritated and impatient. "Come, waiter. Don't be shy."

The waiter looked round the room and took a deep breath. "Tonight," he said, for all to hear, "the Seigneur is dining on frogs' legs and haggis."

A stunned silence was quickly followed by gales of derisive laughter.

"Excellent," said Lady Bertha with apparent relish. "Then that is what I too shall have."

"Very good, my lady." With an inward smirk, the obedient servant took away the unwanted fish and withdrew to fetch Lady Bertha's order.

"Serve you bloody right, Bert," hissed Cissie, who had now decided to rely on bread and wine for sustenance. "Teach you a fucking lesson."

"Cheeky, stuck-up little bitch," snarled her ladyship, aka Bert Pyman, under his breath, and in a pronounced London accent which never failed to make Cissie cringe. "I'll teach *you* a lesson all right when we get upstairs, you see if I don't."

CHAPTER 2

The five-strong party from London had just braved a sea-journey from Colonsay, a small island of the Inner Hebrides – although a good deal larger that Radichsay – in a thirty-foot open boat. The weather for the crossing had been calm and the sea, most unusually, like glass. Having breakfasted early, the travellers were pleasantly animated by the prospect of luncheon at the White Lady Hotel and keenly anticipated the liquid refreshment which would both precede and accompany it. Chrysalis-like, they were ready to shed their outer casing of hats and cloaks and to emerge as butterflies, ready for all that awaited them. At the hotel's private jetty the new arrivals were assisted ashore by two boatmen wearing the white and green livery of the hotel, and were then helped out of their outer garments before entering the white and green painted conservatory which protrudes over a significant portion of the dazzling white beach. Here, the emergent butterflies were greeted obsequiously by Mr Humphrey Bliss – manager and maître d'hôtel. He invited his new guests to be seated at one of the low tables where drinks were taken and from which they would be able to study in detail both the cocktail and wine lists and the luncheon menu. Humphrey Bliss had floppy fair hair, through which he constantly ran a hand, a slender nose and chin, and the petulant mouth of a spoilt six-year old.

The newly arrived travellers would have been horrified had they known that they in turn were the objects of a scrutiny just as keen as their own lists of food and drink on offer. For in a not far distant corner, seated on a low sofa and half hidden behind a Japanese screen, lurked a man who could almost have been a spectre from the hotel's notorious past. With still mostly dark hair parted in the middle and now swept straight back from his high forehead, and slim moustache, the man wore a striped blazer and white flannels; in one eye socket gleamed a rimless monocle and from his mouth protruded a long cigarette-holder which contained an unlighted cigarette. A private detective by profession, the spectral onlooker affected an air of more or less convincing indifference to his surroundings as he sipped his Martini. The conservatory was by no means full and the newly-seated luncheon party made no attempt to keep their voices down, affording the detective little difficulty in hearing what they said.

Mortimer Trippe (for the fashionable figure behind the screen was he) did, however, wonder whether his true purpose might soon be detected by the newcomers. Not only was he on his own in the by no means full room, but he no longer entertained the slightest doubt that the lunch party constituted the Sisterhood whom Lady Bertha had instructed him to watch, and whom she had left him in no doubt were up to no good. Now, from the other side of the Japanese screen, there appeared Mr Humphrey Bliss whose whole approach had about it the manner of someone in no hurry to leave.

Although now generally pleased with his appearance, Mortimer was still sufficiently anxious about it to be glad of anything which might help to deflect possible suspicion. In preparing his disguise Mortimer had been considerably assisted by Mr Lamplighter, and Emily had also done her well-intentioned best. On Mr Lamplighter's advice, Mortimer had started to grow a moustache on his return from Malou a little over two weeks ago (and with no other assignment in mind) as 'they can always be of use in this profession, one way or another, and avoid the all-too-obvious dangers of the false variety'. The moustache had begun life as the full nose-to-lip variety, with commensurate width, but Mortimer had

had it trimmed by an expert to its present slender elegance and was well pleased with the result. The clothes had been the easiest part, readily obtained at a costumier's in a side-street off the Strand. Even the eyeglass, purchased on the advice of the costumier, had been easier to wear than Mortimer had feared. But the hair, even though his own, had given him severe headaches, both figuratively and literally. The costumier's advice that it should be swept straight back and parted in the centre had no doubt been sound in principle and the man could be forgiven for his ignorance of Mortimer's hair's resistance to change. All his life, however, Mortimer had declined the offers of barbers to put 'something' on it. On one occasion, though, many years ago, a new man had done this by stealth, first distracting his customer with an exceptionally tedious disquisition on the merits of a football player of whom Mortimer had never heard and then by nicking his customer's ear in reproof when Mortimer had started to nod off; suddenly the barber had applied the unguent in generous measure when the victim was completely off guard. Mortimer's hair fiercely rebelled against this tactic and, rather than lying flat, had suddenly developed vicious-looking spikes much like those of a porcupine. Mortimer had a longstanding rule never to look in a hairdresser's mirror for fear of what he might see, and it was not until he got home, having been taunted in the street and nearly set upon by a bunch of thugs, that he became aware of the result of the outrage. He looked exactly like a then fashionable punk rocker. This episode had increased Mortimer's vigilance over the years and when some consummate ass had suggested, as a final touch, the application of pomade to his hair Mortimer had initially adamantly refused. He had been prevailed upon, however, by the assurance that such a substance was, in the inter-war period, almost *de rigeur* in the gentleman about town; Mortimer knew that the only hope of persuading his hair to adopt the suggested style was to hold it down by force and this, in suitable quantities, the pomade achieved.

But after hours of practice, and even now in the White Lady Hotel, Mortimer was fearful that his hair might at any moment suddenly spring up and expose him as a sham.

Not until his transformation was perfected in every particular did Mortimer allow Emily so much as a glimpse. She was usually scant in her praise of her husband's appearance, and on her first sighting of his new look, complete with monocle and cigarette-holder, she had not been lost for a derogatory word.

"I don't know what the purpose of all this is, Mortimer, but is the intention to look like a homosexualist?"

Mortimer smiled broadly. "Are you suggesting that I do?"

"Certainly you do. D'you want to invite unwanted attention?"

"Not at all, Emily, but I think that the less, er, normal, I appear the better. I must look neither like myself nor like a private detective. That is the point."

"Well, I think it can be said that you have succeeded admirably in your objective. I just hope that there are no unfortunate consequences. You know as well as I do that you can't tell who's queer and who isn't."

"It doesn't concern me, Emily, and I can't see why it should."

Although Mr Lamplighter's prudence in the matter of confidentiality had ruled out any need for Mortimer to adopt a new name every time that he wished to remain more or less incognito, it was clear that he could not use his own name on this Scottish island, since he might well be following the same people later in the investigation under a different identity – his own, with luck. After considerable thought, and discussion with a doubtful Mr Lamplighter, he had decided on the pseudonym Algernon Jolliffe.

"Could be worse," pronounced Emily grudgingly. "It matches your appearance as near as any name could but with no particular suggestion of pederasty. Thank God you avoided Sebastian."

Now, although it was not the first time that he had been addressed by his adopted name, Mortimer, still nervous behind the Japanese screen, was taken aback when Mr Bliss spoke to him.

"Well, well, Mr Jolliffe, you *do* look snug behind this gorgeous screen." The hotel Manager sat down beside Mortimer on the sofa.

"Yes," said Mortimer, quickly improvising, "there was something of a draught."

Humphrey Bliss clapped his hands and beckoned a minion. "Alasdair, please bring Mr Jolliffe a rug. At once."

Far from being grateful, Mortimer was furious. The rug arrived with exemplary promptitude and was placed over Mortimer's unwilling knees. Mr Bliss moved closer.

"I see what you mean about the draught, Mr Jolliffe – or may I call you Algernon? I feel it myself. Perhaps you would be good enough to allow me to share your rug?" And, uninvited, he drew the rug also over his own knees. Even then Mortimer sensed no danger.

"Don't you find our new guests intriguing, Algernon?" enquired the importunate Humphrey.

"Is there any reason why I should?"

"I myself am fascinated by both the people and their clothes. Were you ever in the rag-trade yourself, Algernon?"

When Mortimer finally realized what was meant by this, he said, "No, no, not at all. Nothing like that. I used to be an accountant. Not certified, you know, chartered."

"*Certified*, my dear! How very restricting. You had a lucky escape. But *chartered*. Like a luxury yacht, my dear. Accessible to all comers, presumably. How *brave* you must be, Algernon." As he said this, he edged closer, but still Mortimer, although he found the man's language extravagant and his behaviour generally irritating, found nothing really amiss.

"Well," said Humphrey Bliss, "now that I have your undivided attention, since we are *trapped*, my dear, in our little nest, I shall share with you some of the expertise of my former profession, and at the same time, perhaps, afford you some insight into the identities and characters of the members of that rather jolly luncheon party, in whom you appeared so interested before I rudely interrupted. Would you like that, Algernon?"

Since Mortimer was here, he assumed, to find out whatever he could about this odd-looking and obviously criminal Sisterhood, this seemed like a Heaven-sent opportunity.

"I should be delighted, Mr Bliss," he said.

"*Humphrey*, my dear, *please*."

"Sorry. Quite. Humphrey."

"That's better, Algernon, much better. We're *chums* now, aren't we?" At this point Mortimer felt, under the rug, some pressure on his thigh, presumably from his 'chum'. He thought little of it, however, but moved slightly away. Humphrey began his commentary, which in Mortimer's opinion was both unnecessarily detailed and protracted.

"The lady who conducted the correspondence before they came was a Miss Elspeth Sturdy. They all have the most *delightful* names. I wonder if they are *genuine*, Algernon."

Here Mr Bliss sniggered and nudged Mortimer provocatively. Was the wretched man hinting that he found Mortimer's own adopted name less than genuine? he wondered guiltily. Perhaps it didn't matter; it sounded right for the period at least.

"I think Miss Sturdy *must* be the lady at the top of the table. She looks like a Sturdy, don't you think, my dear, so *commanding*? She is clearly their *leader*. And aren't they all such darlings, so perfectly turned out. *Very* period, and the *correct* period too, alas far from always the case, but then these days, Algernon, as you know…"

And so it went on, with Humphrey not only, mostly admiringly, describing for 'Algernon's' benefit what all at the low drinks table were wearing but identifying each of them as he went along. For the *full* picture, Humphrey explained,

Algernon would need to remember the party before they took their seats, and those portions of them now invisible.

Miss Sturdy wore an impeccable white Chanel tweed suit with black piping encircling the collar and solid silver buttons down the front of the jacket; various chains and snowy pearls cascaded from her robust neck, whilst her lower extremities, beneath the shortish skirt, boasted striking white silk stockings and black grosgrain Louis-heeled and crossbarred court shoes. The whole ensemble, surmounted by a black cloche felt hat complete with silver buckle on the band, was, in Humphrey's opinion, very nearly faultless. His one reservation was the length of the skirt, which he felt was not *quite* suited either to the lady's undoubted middle age or to the width of her solid country legs, which, he guessed, would be more comfortable in rough tweeds.

On Miss Sturdy's left sat a dark, slim lady of distinctly Mediterranean appearance, who could only be the French lady, Madame Louise Loiseau, clearly determined to compete with her Chanel-suited neighbour in chic, if not in cost. Her jet-black hair was encased in a scarlet turban and highlighted by a dazzling diamond clip. The slender body shimmered in a black wide-legged and wide-sleeved pantsuit, adorned at the front with startling yellow abstract designs, the brainchild, Humphrey surmised, of the Paris couturier who must have known exactly what *Madame* required. Although probably on the brink of attaining *un certain âge*, any suggestion other than that *Madame* still enjoyed the fresh bloom of youth would in Humphrey's humble opinion have seemed not merely insulting but ludicrous.

Humphrey knew that Ollerenshaw is a Northern name and Mrs Gloria Ollerenshaw, black and of ripe but uncertain vintage, was seated opposite Madame Loiseau and addressed her constantly, not only with a beaming smile but in a broad Yorkshire accent. It was evident that when a ravishing appearance was the order of the day, the Yorkshirewoman was not to be outdone. Her dress was of red chiffon with partly visible cream silk lining, plunging front and a zig-zag hemline which formed round the thighs a full circle of alluring (although *not* of course to Humphrey personally – and he giggled with a sideways glance at his new-found 'chum' on the sofa) triangle of gleaming dark flesh. The *pièce de résistance*, however, was a quite extraordinary pattern of bright yellow bananas seemingly dangling from the low-dropped waist and more than a little reminiscent of the erotic dancing of the also black Josephine Baker in her youthful heyday in 1920s Paris. Humphrey, however, found the garment *unspeakably vulgar*. This tawdry item would no doubt have passed muster at some common tea-dance in days gone by or perhaps as fancy dress, but it was *not* suitable for the White Lady. Although he did not say so, Mortimer thought the black woman an absolute corker and her dress easily the most fetching in the room.

Seated at the foot of the table, opposite each other but obviously by no means intimate, there remained two, who could only be Dr Mary Wildegoose and Mr Cyril Jinks. Since both were dressed as men, it was clear from their names that one favoured male attire, and this could hardly be the one of such vast bulk that he had to be, at least technically, male. That must, therefore, be Mr Cyril Jinks and the smaller of the two Dr Mary Wildegoose. (My dear, wasn't this utterly *gripping*!)

Dr Mary looked comfortable in her camel and pale blue check knickerbocker suit, her shapely and supposedly male calves encased in red stockings matching the baggy felt beret, which just failed to cover her over-the-ear length mousy hair. Perhaps by way of counterpoint to this rather audacious outfit she had round her neck an old-style 'choker' accompanied, no doubt suitably, by a regimental tie. She was in Humphrey's opinion the brains of the party. Mr Cyril Jinks was simplicity, if not conventionality, itself, at least in dress. He wore a voluminous pea-green mohair suit and large pink bow-tie, whilst his fingers were bejewelled with colossal stones of uncertain provenance. An honorary woman, my dear, no less. And which side do you suppose *he* bats for? Ours, I think, Algernon, don't you? And Humphrey cackled unrestrainedly. The identification process was complete.

From an extensive list of cocktails the newcomers, except Miss Sturdy, who chose to drink a Virgin Mary, selected the house special, appropriately called White Lady. This, the correct version of the well-known cocktail, the waiter explained, consisted simply of gin, orange liqueur and lemon juice.

When the White Ladies arrived, all who drank them acclaimed their excellence with an enthusiasm corroborated by the speed with which they drank them. Thus pepped up, for these concoctions were not for beginners, the party, except for the abstemious Miss Sturdy, smacked its collective lips and signalled a wish for replenishment. The replenishments were put away with almost equal dispatch and the waiter, who had remained in close attendance, as though more than half-expecting or at least hoping for, this eventuality (for, as Humphrey explained, he was on commission), looked at Miss Sturdy. "The same again, madam?"

"Thank you, waiter. And meanwhile we will make our luncheon selection." All chose lobster salad to start with followed by either venison or beef. As the third and final round of White Ladies was set down on the table, Gloria Ollerenshaw rose from her seat and walked slowly to the centre of the room, now cleared for dancing. There was an expectant hush round the conservatory as she bowed graciously to each corner of the room. Every heterosexual male eye (and indeed the eyes of Dr Mary) now upon her, the black lady said, as if introducing the next turn in a vaudeville: "And now a little number of my own, with apologies to Ogden Nash, if I may, ladies and gentleman, dedicated by a black lady to all White Ladies." This announcement was greeted with somewhat puzzled but enthusiastic applause and Gloria raised her eyes to the ceiling, closed them, folded her hands in front of her like a schoolgirl, and paused dramatically. As she did so, quite suddenly, Mortimer felt a hand on his knee. It could just about be accidental, but Mortimer wasn't so sure now. Could Emily have been right? It was unthinkable. It was not as though he was still a pretty little boy at school, where this sort of thing had not been uncommon, even half-expected. He was a fully grown man, for Heaven's sake! Although Mortimer's mind accepted readily that male homosexuality was a fact, his heart did not. In relation to himself least of all. This *must* be a mistake. He removed the hand with an airy, "Wrong knee, old chap. Natural mistake, I know. Anyone could make it." And he laughed lightly.

Again Humphrey giggled like a teenage girl. "You're such a *tease*, Algy. You really are."

Was this a natural reaction? Mortimer wondered. He realized by now that Humphrey was probably what Emily called a homosexualist, but even so … He just managed to convince himself that nothing untoward was afoot.

Now, in clear ringing tones, Gloria Ollerenshaw began to declaim:

> There is something about a White Lady,
> A tingle remarkably pleasant,
> A whitish a brightish White Lady,
> Ere the feasting and dancing begin,
> And to tell you the truth,
> She is not like Vermouth,
> I think that perhaps she is gin.

This recitation was greeted with thunderous and prolonged applause and loud shouts of 'Encore', but the poetess once more bowed, and returned modestly to her seat. As the waiter took the food order Elspeth Sturdy asked him kindly to inform the *sommelier* that they would accept his recommendations for those wines which most satisfactorily accorded with their food order. This chore complete, attention was directed to the final assault on the third and final round of White Ladies, and glasses were raised with loud cries of yum-yum and other more or less polite marks of appreciation, before the contents were drained and the feasting could begin. And then they moved to the luncheon table.

Only Madame Loiseau was a practised hand in disposing of without fuss or mess a fully intact cold lobster, but the others made up in enthusiasm for what they lacked in finesse. The wine 'went down a treat', as Gloria averred several times in recharging her glass. She explained that the unaccustomed recitation had given her a thirst 'like a Loch Tay salmon', which seemed an appropriate simile in view of their Gaelic surroundings. Elspeth, however, placed a firm hand over her wine glass at the mere sight of the *sommelier* and called imperiously for a jug of tap-water without ice, lemon, maraschino cherries 'or any other nonsense'. She now rapped the table with a knife-handle for silence.

"Fellow writers," she began, and the company fell silent. "We are here to discuss some of the more lamentable and, to us all personally ruinous, aspects of our profession." She now had the attention not only of her immediate audience but seemingly also of those others in the room – a good proportion – whose invariable practice it was to eavesdrop on any conversation not meant for their ears, however tedious. "I refer, of course, to some of the heinous methods of those skunks and scoundrels who dare to call themselves agents and publishers and who sully the name of a once honourable profession." Miss Sturdy went on to expatiate on the greed of agents, the iniquities of publishers' advances, the injustices inherent in the Public Lending Right and so on. It was arid stuff, and her 'fellow writers' made little attempt to conceal the fact that they were bored to distraction. With the arrival of the main course the attention of the Sisterhood again turned to the food. The point, however, had been made. They were serious professional writers. Nothing more, nothing less.

"Now for those *digestifs* as Louise calls 'em," said Gloria, clicking finger and thumb at a waiter. With the coffee, for which they remained at the table, Madame Loiseau, fittingly chose calvados, Mrs Ollerenshaw, also fittingly, Captain Morgan's black rum, Dr Wildegoose port and Mr Jinks Madeira. The same waiter who had so happily served the pre-luncheon cocktails, placed on the table a full bottle of each, hoping no doubt they would do as much justice to these as they had to every other intoxicant which had been placed before them. The fact that the dance-floor now looked like a dance-floor and that a waiter was winding up a magnificent old gramophone, caused Gloria to cry out, "Take your partners." The feasting – though not the drinking – now over, the dancing did indeed begin. Gloria initiated this stage of the proceedings, somewhat improbably, by inviting Cyril Jinks – much to his obvious alarm – to take the floor with her, calling for the Charleston as she did so. At this point Miss Sturdy raised her voice above the sound of the gramophone to announce that for dinner she had secured the private use of the Green Room, where they should all convene for dinner at eight, as there were matters which she wished to discuss.

A private room, thought Mortimer. Damn. Apart from a lot of waffle about writing he hadn't yet heard anything from the Sisterhood worth listening to. And now they were going to have dinner in a private room. That could only mean one thing. That was where they would discuss their plans for whatever outrage they were plotting. And he wouldn't hear a word of it. He couldn't very well have bugged the room even if he had known how to. It looked like the end of the road where his new assignment was concerned. And the whole thing stank: their individual names sounded hardly more genuine than his own; their whole demeanour in the hotel seemed like a deliberate attempt to give a false impression, their dress absurd; that guff about writing was obviously bogus, a cover for what they were really up to. And now a private room. What could he possibly do? But Mortimer's rueful reflections were, perhaps not entirely unexpectedly, but in the most disturbing way imaginable, interrupted. He now felt an alien hand not on his knee, but creeping up his thigh, squeezing and caressing as it went. All his doubts vanished at a stroke. For fear of being overheard he did not dare to speak, but sharply ripped the rug from both his own and his assailant's knees.

"Oh do stop teasing, Algy, please. I know you don't mean it, but it's getting to be a bore."

Mortimer knew that words, even if he had dared to utter appropriate ones in the crowded room, would have no effect, and a thump to the body would only be misconstrued and provoke the blighter further. He had no option. No harder than was warranted by the circumstances, Mortimer biffed Mr Humphrey Bliss on the point of his elegant nose.

CHAPTER 3

"He rang!" Cissie Sykes could hardly contain herself.

"Who rang, for Heaven's sake?" asked Lady Bertha irritably.

"Your detective. Who else knows we're here?"

"I wasn't' aware that *he* knew I was here. *I* certainly didn't tell him."

"Well, he must have guessed. He obviously knew you'd been digging up his past, and where better than the scene of the crime? Barbara answered the phone and you weren't around so I spoke to him myself."

"How kind of you not to trouble me with so trivial a matter, Cissie. And what the – what did he have to say?" Trying to control her anger, Lady Bertha looked around guardedly, but they were still alone, in the hotel's residents' lounge. Not that the room looked like any other hotel lounge on earth, with its original Cézannes, Degas, Matisses and Monets adorning every spare space of oak-panelled wall between the many beamed recesses, and ancient furniture creaking on the bare plank floor; but then in the Castle Hotel little was as expected and, after a while, nothing much a cause for surprise.

"No need to get stroppy, Bert, - er, Bertha," Cissie paused for an effect which was by no means achieved. "Anyway, he's on this Scottish island and the Sisterhood are all there, and Trippe is obviously on the scent."

"So what has he found out? I haven't even told him the main point yet, which is that the Sisters double-crossed me to the tune of nearly two million pounds. You should have let me speak to him, you idiot. Anyway, what has he found out?"

"For a start, that your ugly sisters have hired a private room for dinner so that must be when they're going to do their plotting."

"And my man is invited to this private dinner?" suggested her ladyship with a nasty sneer.

"He hadn't got that far when the phone went dead. He must have been ringing on a public phone, though I can't think why."

"Went dead? What do you mean went dead?"

"Well there was a lot of shouting and a frightful thump, then nothing."

"A thump?"

"More of a clatter, really. It sounded to me as though your sleuth was in a spot of bother."

"I see. I shall just have to wait for the next instalment then, shan't I? And perhaps you'll allow me to speak to him myself next time."

"Certainly, Bertha." Cissie smiled sweetly. "If there is a next time."

"Quite. Now for Christ's sake ring for a drink, before I die of thirst."

As Cissie pressed the service bell, more in hope than any real expectation, two strangers came in. Despite the warm weather the two oldish men wore heavy tweeds and made themselves comfortable in the nearest approximation to armchairs in the room, where they happily discussed their day's ornithological outing, while Lady Bertha and Cissie talked as idly as Bertha's personality would permit of this and that. Soon the bird-fanciers fell into a drowsy silence, the idle chat of the others lost what little momentum it had gathered and likewise dwindled to nothing. Presently one of the tweedy men picked up and glanced at the cover of a glossy magazine called *High Society*. As he let out a cry of "Good God," Cissie Sykes stiffened like a pointer scenting game: but with foreboding.

"Look at this, Alfred. 'High Jinks on Magic Malou', page 1. He turned the page. 'Detectives' Rest and Recreation. Exclusive photo of the Four Eyes Private Enquiry Agency at play. By our roving socialite correspondent Cissie Sykes'." Inset was a photograph of a smugly grinning Cissie, nevertheless looking ravishing.

"Let me see, Bob." There was a pause. Then, "Christ! I see what you mean."

"May I see that, please?" asked Bertha after what she considered a decent interval, and as pleasantly as she was able. Too proud to wear reading glasses, Bertha held the magazine at the full stretch of her arms, thus displaying strong hairy wrists which drew curious looks from the ornithologists and a girlish gasp of alarm from young Sykes. It took her ladyship but seconds to take in the full horror of what she saw. There was a photograph of Mortimer leaning across a bar counter kissing the barmaid with every indication of enthusiasm and surrounded by drunken and importunate women of every type and age, the several nearest of whom he was clawing at indiscriminately. Behind, Mr Lamplighter, his trilby hat askew, was by no means escaping the lascivious attentions of the female throng. What shocked Bertha, however, was not so much the photograph as its provenance. It was perfectly clear to her what had happened. Cissie had seen the photograph while on Malou, probably in the *Malou Mercury*, and sent a copy to this rag in London. They would no doubt have paid her thousands for the exclusive 'right' to use the picture, even though Cissie had not been anywhere near Malou when she was supposed to have taken it. Bertha admitted to herself that the little bitch had been damn clever in using her London connections in this opportunistic, indeed deceitful way. But this time she'd been too clever by three quarters. The Sisterhood knew damn well that Cissie went pretty well wherever Bertha went: Cissie on Malou meant Bertha on Malou. The gaff was blown. They had only to see this – which they would – and Bertha was stuffed. She could of course leave Malou now. But then what? Go into hiding? That wasn't her style. Anyway, if she left, the detective wouldn't be able to get hold of her and she might not be able to contact him. She had by no means given up hope that, whatever the difficulties, he would find out about whatever the bloody Sisters were plotting. Bertha had faith in the Four Eyes Private Enquiry Agency and who could blame them for letting their hair down a bit after a notable success. Damn Cissie, all the same. The older woman sometimes wondered why she put up with the stupid cow. Bertha might have wondered that, but Bert knew exactly why.

* * *

In a dense and dripping wood – where a heavy Hebridean downpour ensured that even the thickest of the foliage afforded little protection – Mortimer Trippe sprawled in the leaves of last autumn, still dazed. His head ached from a bump – probably against a tree stump – and he groped in the undergrowth for his suitcase which he remembered being hurled after him through the roofed back-gate far up the steep White Lady garden, through which he had been propelled before being knocked insensible. When his hands found the case, it was burst wide open, the contents sodden.

Desperately, he looked round. The thick wood fell sharply almost to the shore. In the distance, the sea was calm but speckled by the lashing rain. But what was that? Could it be? Two forms were sporting in the water. Mortimer rubbed his eyes, but the apparitions were still there: nymphs or mermaids with flowing blonde hair gracefully slicing the water; sirens perhaps, like the Lorelei, waiting to lure fishermen onto the rocks, not of the Rhine, but of Radichsay Bay. Watching, Mortimer was entranced. Soon these fabulous creatures began to swim towards the shore; moments later they stood up, laughing and splashing, and waded towards the beach. Both were quite, quite naked. Mortimer decided that he must be dreaming; more likely, it was that blow to the head. He closed his eyes and took deep breaths; he counted slowly up to ten; he shook his head and opened his eyes. They were gone! Perhaps to that divine place whence they had come; more probably, they had never existed. Mortimer sighed. But wait! A blonde head appeared, and then another. As they emerged from the sand dunes, Mortimer saw that they were now dressed. They were nuns! Each wore a glistening white habit, adorned with a single yellow cross over the heart and their hands were piously folded in front of them.

Mortimer could not go back to the White Lady, there were no boats and he had nowhere to stay and nothing to eat. Could these extraordinary sisters be a means of salvation? He had nothing to lose and called out. There was no reaction. He called again, louder. The nuns halted in their tracks and looked at one another. One pointed up at the wood and they quickened their pace. As they entered the wood they used their hands to climb and their eyes searched the thicket for a sign of humankind. Mortimer quickly stuffed most of his belongings back into his case, shut it with difficulty and stumbled down through the thick growth towards the young women, calling out, "Here I am. I'm coming. Hello! Hello! Thank you." When victim and rescuers finally met, Mortimer found the encounter both surprising and pleasant. Far from being of a silent order, the two nuns chattered away like schoolgirls – a far cry from what Mortimer would have expected from the inhabitants of the hallowed cloisters in which they presumably lived.

"Well you are in a pickle," said one. "Just look at him, Sister Serenity."

"I'm not blind, Sister Mercy," snapped Sister Serenity before turning to Mortimer. "Whatever happened to you, you poor old thing?"

Mortimer explained that he had been manhandled and thrown out of the hotel on the express orders of the proprietor, just as he was making an important telephone call.

"I say, how exciting! I'm longing to know what he did, aren't you, Sister Serenity?"

"We live a sheltered life here, you see," explained Sister Serenity. "And this is quite the most thrilling thing either of us can remember, isn't it, Sister Mercy?"

"Yes, but," Sister Mercy fixed Mortimer with a wide and innocent blue eye, "What did you do?"

"I punched Mr Bliss on the nose."

The nuns cheered in unison, and then squealed, "Wow!" "Good for you," "What did *he* do?"

"He was becoming importunate."

There was silence as the young ladies tried to grasp the significance – or even the meaning – of this, but Mortimer had no intention of being more explicit.

Now Sister Mercy asked eagerly, "Did you draw blood?" Sister Serenity was deep in thought.

"Yes. He seemed to bleed easily. He got quite hysterical actually."

"Good. Bit of a queer fish, Mr Bliss, so we've heard."

"Very queer," said Mortimer with feeling.

Sister Serenity had now recovered her speech. "That long word you used – er, by the way, what's your name?"

"Mortimer Trippe."

"That word – did it mean what you read in the *News of the World* about men importing – importuning – in public lavatories?"

"More or less."

"Gosh!"

"Golly!"

"I hope you bashed him really hard," said Sister Mercy, giggling.

"No harder than I had to."

But Sister Serenity looked concerned. "Don't tell Himself that, Mr Trippe. He can't stand this Bliss bloke and he'll think you a hero to have biffed him on the snout, but he won't reckon much if you say it wasn't that hard."

"Himself?"

"The Laird."

"The Thane."

"The Captain."

"The Chieftain."

The sisters spoke in awe.

"We're taking you to him," explained Sister Mercy. "He'll help you, Mr Trippe. You need help, don't you?"

"Yes," said Mortimer, "I do."

It appeared to have stopped raining now and one of these angels picked up Mortimer's suitcase, the other waved an arm in the opposite direction from the White Lady, and they set off.

CHAPTER 4

Deep inside the cool marble bar in the Old Brompton Road, properly called the Friar Tuck but now abbreviated by Emily Trippe and Annie Hoare to 'the Friar', the two discursive Kensington women were again seated on opposite sides of a litre of house white. After a lively discussion about the merits and otherwise of that perfectly maddening restaurant in Sydney Street which kept changing its name, the unbelievable new clothes shop in High Street Ken where it was actually possible to walk round without being half-deafened by so-called music, and other pressing issues of the day, Annie suddenly plucked from her handbag, somewhat in the manner of a magician producing a rabbit from a top hat, a neatly folded full page cut-out from a glossy magazine called *High Society*, which she handed to Emily. It was the same piece, including photograph, which Bertha had more or less snatched from one of the tweedy bird-fanciers in the Castle Hotel. "What on earth is this?" she demanded.

"Oh, just a holiday snap," Annie said, trying to conceal her amusement at the surprise in store for Emily, who mysteriously seemed not yet to have grasped the significance of the thing.

"But what of?" asked Emily irritably.

"Malou, of course. The photograph speaks for itself, I should have thought. It's from a mag called *High Society*. A sort of downmarket *Tatler*. Rather fun."

Emily peered at it. Not having her reading glasses with her, she could not read what was written and the photograph was little more than a blur, although she could make out two men in what looked to be highly compromising positions surrounded by a host of semi-naked women; unless Emily was mistaken one of the men was kissing a very décolletée barmaid. "Why should I be interested in this kind of sordid rubbish, for Christ's sake, Annie?"

Annie was still mystified. "Doesn't anything about it – er, strike you, so to speak, Emily?"

"Well I confess that the lecher at the bar *does* look somehow – almost hauntingly familiar. But apart from that, no."

At this point their waiter, never far away, made a sign to the barman who produced an old cigar box and handed it to the waiter, who said to Emily, as he placed the box on her table, "Forgive me, Madam, but some of our elderly customers find these useful." The box contained a number of pairs of forgotten reading glasses. Overlooking with difficulty the use of the word 'elderly', Emily tried on and discarded several pairs before finding one which would serve the purpose. She read the words and examined the photograph and turned successively white, pink, red and finally mauve in the face. She was unable to speak, but simply slammed the offending cutting onto the table, although careful not to tear it up. It might come in useful.

"I thought it might interest you," said Annie archly.

"And who, might I ask, is this Cissie Sykes?"

"God, her. I'm surprised you haven't heard of her. What they used to call a bit fast. Always getting into the gutter press one way or another."

"I think," said Emily, "that there's more to this than meets the eye."

"Plenty meets the eye as it is," replied her friend with an uncharacteristically straight face.

Emily swallowed what was left of her drink, poured the remnants of the bottle into her glass and clicked her fingers at the waiter.

With Sister Serenity in front and Sister Mercy bringing up the rear, Mortimer's gait through the dense foliage was halting and stumbling compared with the graceful movements of his accompanying angels. After some twenty minutes he suddenly saw through the gradually thinning wood a towering granite fortress. It consisted of two huge turret-like structures, apparently Norman, each surmounted by battlements, and attached to one another only by a long, low edifice which looked from the distance to be of a later period and was roughly the shape and size of a large mediaeval tithe-barn. Mortimer knew from a map hanging in the hotel that this was Fort Radich. Now, in the lightening sky and surrounded by juniper, Scots pine and yew, it looked majestic. Soon they were on a track leading over a blasted heath dotted with wild scarlet pimpernels, snow-white sheep munching, and long-haired, long-horned Highland cattle doing the same but with the occasional blank stare at the visitors. And a lone and splendid black stallion.

As they moved on, Mortimer thought about the Laird, or Thane, or Chieftain, or whatever he was: Himself. A ruffian by reputation and by no means a good egg; probably more at home in his native Gaelic than in English, if indeed he had any real command of the latter language at all. Mortimer was curious. The sisters had not spoken since they set off but as they approached the Fort Mortimer sensed a mounting excitement in his companions, although, hands now once more piously folded in front of them, they could almost have been from a silent order. Had he imagined the schoolgirl slang and chatter of barely half an hour ago?

On arrival, a massive oak door confronted them in the middle of the Fort's central building; on it was a large iron knocker in the form of a stag's head. With the easy assurance of a regular visitor, Sister Serenity took hold of one antler and delivered three resounding thumps which eventually brought out an impassive, unshaven and unfriendly fellow with a squat nose and a squint.

"Hello, Hector. Himself here?" asked Sister Serenity. Without replying, the man nodded wordlessly to the interior and walked ahead.

"Not *quite* as bad as he looks," Sister Mercy told Mortimer, "though not far off. One of a couple of MacRadich servants. The other one, Andy, is more or less bats. All inter-related of course."

"Not easy to get staff, I suppose," giggled Sister Serenity. They were back on their old form.

Hector led them into a curious room at the edge of a courtyard. It was hovel-like and wretched: no curtains, no soft chairs – certainly no cushions – no pictures or flowers, no outside window and not scrupulously clean.

"We're looking for Himself, as I said." Sister Serenity was beginning to sound irritable.

Hector grunted and withdrew, returning a few moments later to tell the uninvited guests what he must already have known. "Abed," he said and once more left the room.

"Don't worry, Mr Trippe," said Sister Mercy. "Himself always has a siesta." She glanced at an ancient and dusty grandfather clock. "He'll be here in a minute or two, just you see."

And so he was. Barefooted, wearing a garish kilt ablaze with red and green, his shirt sleeves were rolled up showing muscular arms despite his apparently being nearer seventy than sixty; he had a lined and craggy face surmounted by fiery red hair which matched not only that of his arms and legs but the red in his kilt. The impression of a ruffianly fellow was not lessened by his curt nod by way of greeting. Over his shirt he wore a garment which puzzled Mortimer; it was a short-sleeved cricket sweater bearing the colours of Magdalen College, which Mortimer easily recognized, having himself often turned out for his own Oxford college side, if only as twelfth man and scorer. Had the old Scot pinched the sweater or found it somewhere? The puzzle was solved as soon as the Laird opened his mouth.

"Well, hello, girls. What a delightful surprise. Aren't you going to introduce me to your friend?"

"Hi, Gus," said the sisters, more or less in unison. They looked at Mortimer and then doubtfully at each other. "Shall I tell Himself?" asked Sister Serenity. "You're inclined to cut corners."

Sister Mercy nodded reluctantly and Sister Serenity, having first introduced Mortimer, launched into a breathless account of the rescue operation and what had necessitated it.

"Christ, you poor chap. I always knew that bugger Bliss needed some sorting out. Don't worry about a thing, my dear fellow, I'll soon fix him." The sisters nudged each other as Himself paused. "Now, Trippe, presumably your main wish is to get back into the hotel and resume your holiday?"

Mortimer thought quickly. There was something about Himself which made the detective sense that the Chieftain might be able to help in an even more important way, though Mortimer had no specific idea how. Without disclosing his purpose, he explained that he should have been at an important meeting in the hotel at seven o'clock that evening, that the other participants were leaving by private boat immediately afterwards and that he needed to know what was said at the meeting by nine o'clock that night at the latest. The only way of achieving this would be to have the meeting tape recorded so that he could listen to the recording on his return to the hotel and in time for his deadline. In suggesting this course of action, he said, he was assuming that it would take some little time after Mr Bliss's own return to the hotel – assuming that was, that he would be coming here – before suitable arrangements could be made for he himself to re-enter the establishment, given the violence of his earlier ejection and the obviously high feelings attending it. Even as he spoke Mortimer knew that this story was riddled with improbabilities, but Himself grinned complicitly, picked up a huge old service revolver from a small table, walked half into the courtyard and fired twice into the air. The loud reports caused Mortimer to start violently but the two nuns, who had presumably witnessed this performance before, remained apparently unsurprised and impassive.

"Sorry about that," said the Laird as he resumed his seat, but Hector's a bit deaf. Only thing he hears."

Hector was in the room in a trice, just as sullen as when the visitors arrived.

"Can you hear me, MacRadich Major?" shouted the 24th Captain of Clanradich.

"Ugh."

"Good. I want that worm Bliss from the hotel. Bring him here. Now. Got it?"

"Ugh." And Hector MacRadich left to do his master's bidding.

While they were waiting, Himself and Mortimer talked about London, which Himself now only occasionally visited, usually staying at the Caledonian Club but, if he wanted 'a yarn', then at the Special Forces Club in Knightsbridge.

Half an hour later Humphrey Bliss was standing in the room, held at the scruff of his neck by his uncouth captor and shaking violently. He looked appealingly at 'Algernon' but Mortimer wisely did not meet his eye. Himself explained to Humphrey what was wanted but Mr Bliss said nothing.

Now Himself picked up a large hand-bell which rested beside the revolver and waved it above his head. This time it brought forth a dim-looking fellow built like an ox.

"Ah, MacRadish Minor" – the Laird turned to Mortimer – "Sorry if this jargon reminds you of school but I'm blessed if I know what else to call the blighters." He turned back to the dimwit. "Strip the prisoner to the waist, gag him and lash him to the plane tree."

Struggling feebly and squealing loudly, Humphrey was unceremoniously stripped to the waist and tied tightly by the wrists, his arms almost encircling the trunk of a plane tree in the courtyard. Just as he seemed to have found the power of speech, a handkerchief was thrust into his mouth and an Old Etonian tie bound round his jaw to keep the gag in place. Mortimer was already beginning to feel uneasy when the dimwit produced from a small shed a vicious looking scourge. 'MacRadish Minor', now himself also stripped to the waist and displaying a torso which did indeed resemble that of a shot-putter, began to swish the instrument of punishment viciously in the air with every appearance of relish. Mortimer had followed Himself into the courtyard, but Sisters Serenity and Mercy had now disappeared almost as mysteriously as they had emerged from the sand dunes. Mortimer turned to Himself in protest but received in reply only a huge wink.

"Twenty-four of the best," said Himself to the dimwit, who grinned like an alligator, "unless we need more, that is, which I somehow doubt. When I give the order. Now, Bliss, are you prepared to do as I ask?" He explained Mortimer's requirements.

The wretched Humphrey nodded his head as vigorously as his situation would allow.

"Period for reflection," announced Himself to no one in particular, nodding to Mortimer and the two MacRadich servants to follow him inside, and leaving Mr Humphrey Bliss, proprietor of the renowned White Lady Hotel, to ponder his fate.

"You like horses?" the Laird asked Mortimer, who replied equivocally but was nonetheless given a guided tour of the stables. After ten minutes or so Himself indicated that it was time to review the situation in the courtyard. Humphrey took little convincing that if he did not do as Himself had ordered, the next session would be no dress rehearsal. Another two shots from the revolver brought Hector back and he was ordered to return the hotelier whence he had brought him. As Humphrey was led away, relief written all over his face, Himself made it clear to him that the abused hotel guest would be returning in a couple of hours at the outside, when everything and everyone should be ready for his reception, including the tape recorder awaiting his convenience. Mortimer had the impression that Humphrey would have surrendered the remainder of the hotel lease there and then in order to get away.

"Bit of time to kill, then, Mortimer, eh? A dram or two, I think."

And a dram 'or two' it was. The chat, as happens on these occasions, became increasingly relaxed and soon from relaxed to matey and finally almost festive as reminiscences were exchanged. Time passed quickly, and when it was reluctantly judged that it was time for the guest to leave, Mortimer's first attempts to stand up were not wholly successful. Again two shots rang out from the courtyard and Hector was ordered once more, as he doubtless saw it, to half-carry and half-drag an unsteady Sassenach through the woods to the unholy White Lady Hotel.

Somewhat to Mortimer's surprise, Humphrey was waiting for him at the back-gate of the hotel garden. With a muttered, "at last," the hotelier led him inside. Mortimer was still far from steady on his feet and was happy to be shown in through the tradesman's entrance at the rear of the hotel. He was grateful for Humphrey's discretion and didn't really bear the fellow a grudge; after all, Mortimer supposed, the chap had no doubt, for him, probably behaved quite normally. Mortimer reflected, indeed, that if Emily was right, he himself might even inadvertently have supplied some encouragement, weird and vexing though the whole episode had unquestionably been. And he could hardly blame Humphrey for behaving so cravenly in the Fort's courtyard; he would probably have been no more resolute himself at the prospect of twenty-four of that dimwit brute's best!

Mortimer followed his erstwhile importuner to the Green Room, where the tape-recorder was now lined up for him on a shining mahogany table. Humphrey showed him how to work the thing, assured him that he would not be disturbed as the 'Private – Do Not Disturb' sign was still in place, and left him alone. Mortimer and machines of any kind did not make natural bedfellows, but this gadget seemed almost childishly simple, even for someone of Mortimer's limited technical expertise: 'play' and 'stop' buttons were simple enough, and one for forward, another for back to rewind, a fast forward button to hear a section again and a delete button for when you'd finished; also, of course, a volume control. And that was it. Even with all that whisky inside him, Mortimer could see no problem and he was very much looking forward to hearing what the bossy Miss Sturdy had had to say, for he had little doubt that it was she who would be doing the talking. He was right. As soon as he pressed the play button that forbidding schoolma'am's voice filled the room as it must have done at the private dinner. Quickly, if unnecessarily, he turned down the volume. To the point of inaudibility as it happened, but he soon redressed that. This should reveal all about their dastardly plot, Mortimer told himself, and he would now have something to report to this Lady Bertha female. Concentrate on the tape, Mortimer, he told himself: you've already missed the first bit; probably just introductory guff though, and he could always play it again; in fact he'd probably play the whole damn thing several times, so that he could savour it and memorize it before erasing it. He listened.

"...at all events, Sisters..." Sisters! Good Heavens! As if those delicious creatures from the sea weren't still occupying half of his admittedly at present slightly imperfect mind as it was. How dare these dashed crooks compare themselves with such perfection? "...two absolutely crucial matters," droned the recorder. "First the question of Lady Bertha remains unresolved. I need hardly stress the importance of her not being allowed to interfere with Phase Two of the Project in the abominable way which caused us to abort Phase One. The other matter is, of course, the implementation of Phase

Two. Before I address these vital issues, however …" Blah, blah, thought Mortimer. He was so anxious to get to the nub, or rather the two nubs, of the thing that his finger hovered over the fast forward button, but he resisted the temptation.

Just as the schoolma'am seemed to be getting to the point, there was a knock at the door. Never mind, Mortimer told himself, you can always replay it, you've got all night and you'd better have another listen in the morning as well, when the head's cleared a bit. Without thinking to press the stop button, he went to the door, where, having no recollection of ordering anything, he was vaguely surprised to see a waiter bearing on a silver tray a bottle of Scotch whisky, a cut-glass jug of water and an agreeably capacious glass. He let the man in and the supplies were placed on a sideboard. Mortimer graciously handed the waiter a five-pound note, waved away his thanks, poured a Himself-sized measure and returned to the recorder.

"…and now, Sisters, to the second issue, the implementation of Phase Two…" Great, thought Mortimer, here it comes, the *pièce de résistance*. Something else to savour over as many re-plays as he wished. Sisters again, though! What a difference! He began to hum: "She'll be coming round the mountain when she comes, she'll be wearing next to nothing when she comes…" Had he missed something out? Oh, well. He turned back to the tape-recorder. "…so there we are. Are there any questions?" To hell with questions, thought Mortimer. He decided to start again from the beginning and this time to *concentrate*. The thing whizzed back at Mortimer's command and when it stopped, he pressed the fast forward button. He decided to have a sip of whisky. But it wasn't there. Damn, he'd left the glass on the sideboard. By the time he'd got back to the table the tape should be getting towards the end. It was, and he pressed the stop button. Now for it! He pressed 'play'. That was odd. He couldn't hear a thing. He turned up the volume. Still nothing. Mortimer felt a twinge of doubt. Then a surge. Had he pressed the wrong button? Even in his present state surely he couldn't have been such a clot as to have pressed the delete button. He couldn't have wiped off the whole tape: it would defeat the very purpose of his coming to this blasted island. It would nullify his ingenuity in his elaborate lie to Himself to enlist his help; and would render futile Himself's gallant efforts to persuade Humphrey to do the necessary. He simply couldn't have obliterated the very thing that would have given some purpose to his visit! He *couldn't* have.

But he had.

CHAPTER 5

'The Beak' sat in the train bound for Hereford looking out at a very different scene from those he was used to in the drearier districts of East London. Most of the way since leaving Paddington, particularly after Oxford, his eyes had feasted on the most glorious of English countryside.

The landscape was in sharp contrast, too, to the place of his birth, of which he himself had almost no recollection, although he knew about it well enough from his parents, and about the horrors of life under Soviet rule. His parents had first moved away from their original home in Tallinn in the hope of finding work, and had chopped and changed before ending up in Kohtla-Järve, a dismal industrial town at the heart of Estonia's oil-shale mining district not far from the Russian border. Here his father had worked underground and in dreadful conditions for a pittance right up until the Great Escape. The town was encircled by man-made slag heaps which had gradually grown to rank among the highest hills in Estonia. It was like a completely different planet from what the Beak now saw from the train window; the very signs at the small railway stations as well as the road signs in the distance betokened a magical and perhaps unknowable world: Charlbury, Shipton-under-Wychwood, Kingham, Moreton in Marsh…

Across the aisle, the Beak's companions sat at a table, taking swigs from a bottle of vodka. They were more than companions, they not only shared his Baltic origins but all five of them effectively shared a common genesis, a common coming to life, for the first clear recollection of every single one of them was the Great Escape in that small open boat in a terrifying rainstorm and at night, so that they could hardly see: an escape first across the Gulf in the dark to Finland; and eventually, weeks later, to their new home – England, London the start of a different existence.

The vodka-drinkers comprised three other young men and a young woman, she as blonde-haired as the men were dark. One of the men held on his knee a kannel, a version of the zither, but they continued to drink in silence. Just outside Charlbury the train slowed down and stopped short of the station. After ten minutes or so there was a barely audible announcement which, of the Estonians, only the Beak heard.

"We've had a collision with a couple of wood-pigeons and we came off second-best," he announced laconically in a noticeable London accent. Shortly, some sort of official came into the carriage and started asking everyone their destination. Soon after that there was a more audible announcement over the tannoy – to the accompaniment of universal groans – saying that due to the 'incident on the line' the train would be going no further and 'customers' were being asked to make the rest of their journeys by road. The passengers were herded out of the train, whence it was necessary to walk the hundred yards or so to the pretty little station. Soon swarming all over the car-park, the people from the train were assembled into groups according to their destinations and asked to await the 'early arrival' of coaches so that they would be able to continue their journeys in comfort. Scorning such regimentation the Estonian party went into the waiting room and sat down.

In the car park those awaiting their transport grumbled, looked at their watches, peered down the road and exchanged listless talk. No coach arrived. After some forty minutes they heard a strange sound from the waiting-room: a loud chord strummed on some alien instrument. Out of boredom and curiosity, some began to trickle into the waiting-room. There a haunting contralto, backed by two tenors and a deep bass, like that of an Orthodox priest, filled the room. The group was conducted by a tall man with a huge beak of a nose, now wearing a shining black cloak and top-hat. As the sound of the ancient Estonian ballad – telling of the legend of some pre-Christian hero – waxed and grew, more people pressed their way into the waiting-room until it was packed, and soon the audience thronged onto the platform. There were more ballads and epic songs, most now, in the Estonian tradition, unaccompanied. There were mutterings that coaches were arriving in considerable numbers, but the mutterers were waved and hushed to silence.

When the performance was over, the Beak took off his hat and bowed. "We are 'The Chameleons'," he said simply, and passed the hat round.

When apparently satisfied that the generosity of the audience had been exhausted, the Beak returned to his group and, at vehement popular request, conducted an encore. By way of finality he announced, in his clear East London voice, "Another train will come shortly. They have no choice. You see."

And ten minutes later another train, quite empty, pulled up at the platform.

* * *

When Elspeth Sturdy arrived at Malou Airport to carry out the first part of her plan she was still pale and trembling from the flight on the small Island Hopper from Jersey. It took a lot to shake Elspeth but, where many had failed, the funny little foreign-sounding pilot, with his frantic non-stop commentary and his idiosyncratic flying methods, had succeeded. On the approach to Malou, when the pilot had aimed his craft directly at a point some forty feet below the top of a cliff face in order to take advantage of a strong upward air current, which would otherwise have made any possibility of landing at all quite out of the question, even the staunchest atheists among his passengers had offered up supplications for deliverance. On arrival Elspeth was the first to reach the taxi-rank, or what passed for one, and was approached by a driver and asked if he could help.

"Yes, I have an appointment with the Seigneur, as a matter of fact, although no time has been arranged for it. I'm staying at the Castle Hotel but I don't want to go there until I've seen the Seigneur."

There was a good reason for this. Lady Bertha was still at the Castle Hotel which was next to Malou Castle, where the Seigneur lived, and Elspeth had no wish to see or be seen by her ladyship until after the business with the Lord of the Island. The letter in her handbag purporting to be from the Home Office, was intended to contrive the removal of Lady Bertha Hook to somewhere nice and safe for the time being and Elspeth knew that the mere sight of one of her former accomplices would put Bertha on the alert. The official looking letter in fact owed as much to good fortune as to Elspeth's ingenuity. It happened that the Sisterhood's confidential secretary in London (the one whom Lady Bertha still kept 'sweet') had formerly worked for the Home Office, and had had the foresight to keep for possible future use a supply of printed Home Office notepaper.

From what the Chief Sister had been able to find out about the workings of the anomalous government in Malou, it seemed that its system of criminal justice was more independent of the British authorities than was the civil government of the Island, which owed ultimate allegiance to the British Crown; and since also the ultimate civil authority on Malou was the Seigneur – whilst all final authority in criminal matters was vested in the Attorney-general, which position was at present vacant – it seemed that the correct entity to whom to address her request was Seigneur de Lessay himself. Elspeth had the previous day posted to this gentleman the original of her letter, which she had personally typed and which was signed in a scrawl apparently by a junior Home Office minister. The posts to Malou were reputedly wretched, but if the letter had not already arrived Elspeth thought that an element of surprise would be no bad thing; if her arrival caught de Lessay on the hop, where was the harm? She herself was well prepared and could easily explain to the feudal lord all that was necessary in order to achieve her objective. She asked to be taken to Malou Castle, but for the taxi-driver to drop her suitcase off at the hotel.

The Castle itself had a forbidding square façade with small, barred windows and no means of entry save across a creaking drawbridge and through a massive oak metal-studded portal protected by a highly unreliable looking portcullis; now raised but threatening, it seemed to Elspeth, to crash down at any moment on the unwary like a rusting guillotine. She flitted as lightly as possible across the drawbridge, thanking Providence that she did not have the additional weight of a suitcase with her, for she had never learned to swim. The now thoroughly unnerved visitor pulled tentatively on a bell-chain, while glancing up occasionally and uneasily at the portcullis. Although she dimly heard a resounding clang from the other side of the door, nothing happened. She waited. Still nothing. She pushed, and to her surprise the door groaned open. She must, she realized, appear like a criminal. It was almost pitch dark inside. And then suddenly a figure appeared, holding an oil-lamp aloft. To Elspeth's unspeakable horror, she could just make out that the figure was a bearded woman. By now quite ready to flee, the Chief Sister was arrested by the sound of a booming male voice with a distinct Scots accent. The man undoubtedly wore a beard but he was also wearing a kilt! Thank God at least for that, thought the usually intrepid visitor. Out of the gloom she suddenly heard another voice, a man again, but this time with an educated English accent. As the second figure came closer she could see that he was quite elderly and wearing a three-piece tweed suit which looked as though it had been in long service.

"Forgive me for the rather unconventional welcome," the man said. "I am Guy de Lessay. It is seldom that anyone beards me in my den."

Was this a rebuke? Elspeth wondered. If it was, it was just too bad. She introduced herself, saying that she was on business from the Home Office in London.

"Good. Excellent. I wasn't expecting you for another week or so, as a matter of fact, but do come in."

Mystified, Elspeth followed the Seigneur into a high-vaulted chamber which, she was relieved to see, was properly lighted by electricity. The first man had disappeared without speaking but, again without speaking, he now brought in a tray bearing a decanter of whisky, a jug of water and two glasses, and placed it on the desk at which host and guest were now seated. With an apology for the absence of choice but no other comment, the Seigneur poured two glasses of whisky and water and looked at Elspeth.

"To progress," he said, raising his glass, and Elspeth echoed his words even as a piece of crumbling masonry fell between them. "So you have come about our modest prison improvements," said the Lord of the Island, "which I need hardly say, are long overdue." He looked at her.

"Well – I – not exactly. It's more about –"

"We do not, of course, need authorization or anything like that from you people, but we shall be grateful for your advice. I don't know whether you saw the existing prison on your way in from the airport, but it is little bigger than a dog kennel."

Elspeth realized that they appeared to be very much at cross-purposes, but with a mumbled apology, she pushed her letter across the desk to her host, who read it briefly.

"Lady Bertha seems to have committed some quite appalling offences," said the Seigneur with a puzzled expression. The letter said that, although at this stage it was merely a request, Scotland Yard wished to make further enquiries before an arrest could be made and, in view of the very real fear of abscondence, the Home Office would be greatly obliged to the Government of the Island if the suspect could be temporarily incarcerated within the Island's jurisdiction pending the outcome of the police enquiries.

"It is essentially a case of an informal government-to-government request, Seigneur," purred Sister Elspeth.

"I see. Well, if I can help – though it does sound rather odd – then perhaps we can get on with the other matter, eh?"

"Certainly," said Elspeth, who realized that the Seigneur was not interested in the Home Office request and only wanted to pursue his own project for prison improvement or whatever it was.

The Seigneur scratched his jaw and looked up at the ceiling far above him. "Well I can hardly detain a member of the English nobility in what is little more than a dog kennel, even for a short time. It would not be seemly." He pressed a bell and scribbled something at the bottom of Elspeth's letter. The kilted man returned. "Ah, Angus. Please give this letter to Sergeant Stockdale at once and tell him to bring the person concerned here forthwith. Also the matter is to be treated in the strictest confidence. The Scotsman nodded, took the letter and withdrew. De Lessay turned to his guest. "Lady Bertha will have to spend her internment here. It is secure if not very comfortable, although probably no worse than the hotel. I hope the lady enjoys haggis." He looked enquiringly at Elspeth, who shrugged. "Angus's culinary range is limited, I fear, but I came quite to enjoy the dish after my first ten years or so north of the border. Now I eat little else."

"That sounds most satisfactory," said Elspeth. "Thank you."

"It's the least I can do, Madam. So that is settled. Now, the important question of the new penal facilities. The present ones are primitive, where they are not actually non-existent." Again he looked briefly at the vaulted ceiling. "You would hardly believe it," he said, now looking at Elspeth with his most earnest expression, "but when I returned after many years from voluntary exile, I even had to build my own guillotine."

* * *

Although the small country town of Hay-on-Wye lies mostly in Wales – but partly in England – and although the local accent is Welsh, even if the ancient Celtic language is itself not spoken here, the place has paradoxically been described as the very epicentre of English eccentricity. Unquestionably it has for many years been internationally renowned for its many second-hand bookshops and it has recently acquired an almost equal celebrity because of its annual literary festival – no longer a humble book fair – which appeals to literati and glitterati of every kind, but for the most part from London. Certainly nobody in the top ranks of the media would risk not being seen on the occasion.

The festival was in full swing. One of the events – a welcome respite from books and authors – was to be held in the Castle garden and had been billed as chamber music by a string quartet from Estonia. When the audience assembled in the enclosed and book-lined garden, however, their eyes focused inevitably on a gleaming white baby-grand piano standing on an otherwise empty podium. Somehow it looked more appropriate for the accompaniment of a dance-band or for some sort of very middle-brow performance in a private club or luxury hotel. But for a string quartet? Perhaps it was destined for some quite different event. When a tall man wearing a shining black cloak and top-hat, with what looked like a large false nose, entered from the street, however, followed by four members of his ensemble, a bright blonde woman among black-haired men all wearing scarlet, doubt turned to certainty. There must have been some terrible mistake!

Faint hope rose tentatively when the musicians produced from behind a curtain a bass, a cello and a violin but as, conducted flamboyantly by the man in the top-hat, the quartet began to play, all hope was soon dashed. Although they started with *Eine Kleine Nazchtmusik*, the selection deteriorated through waltzes and polkas to *Moon River*, *La Vie en Rose* and similar vulgarities until finally the *élite* audience was obliged to sit through *Tipperary* and – the most insulting of all – *Roll out the Barrel*. The assembled gathering of music-lovers were too well-mannered to resort to booing, but did permit themselves a slow hand clap. It seemed, however, that these foreign musicians misconstrued this, for, to widespread horror, it provoked them to even further excesses of vulgarity.

There was fierce muttering among the audience, largely induced by the belief that the whole outrage must be a supposed joke, in the worst possible taste. Did the Estonians perhaps have a very peculiar sense of humour?

But the ultimate affront was yet in store, for when the music died down the man with the nose came round with his hat, grinning broadly and offering anticipatory thanks for all offerings.

CHAPTER 6

"Where's Lady Bertha Hook?"

"Have you seen Lady Bertha?"

Cissie Sykes had not been able to get any sense out of anyone at the hotel, but after asking everyone else she could think of, she finally alighted on Barbara, the pretty young hotel dogsbody, just returning from shopping. In spite of her still humble position, Barbara acted as the eyes and ears of the place, but even she knew nothing. She did, however, do her best.

"Have you tried the nick?"

"The nick? No. Should I have?"

"She wouldn't be the first of our guests to have ended up there. The gaoler likes a bit of company, you see."

So Cissie tried the prison.

"Nothing doing," she told Barbara when she got back.

"Ask Barney Stockdale then. The local police big-shot. He ought to know."

But he didn't. That someone on the Island should have gone missing – and a titled person at that – without him hearing a dickybird greatly offended both his self-esteem and his professional pride. "Just you leave it to me," he said, ogling young Cissie from top to toe and up to top again with extreme lasciviousness. "You can count on me, Miss."

But she couldn't. All the sergeant found out after apparently intensive enquiries was that Lady Bertha Hook had disappeared. "I've put her on our Missing Persons Register," he told Cissie helpfully. He did not tell her that Lady Bertha was the first and quite likely the last person ever to be placed on this register.

"A fat lot of good that will do," snorted Cissie contemptuously. Barney had never in his whole professional career been treated by anyone even half-sober in such a way. "A bit of respect, Miss, if you please."

"Oh piss off you, pompous bastard," said Cissie, leaving the chief of the Malou police open-mouthed. But where could she turn now? The Seaview bar was full of gossip all right, but that's all it was: gossip and rumour. She wanted hard facts. Barbara had done her best, but Cissie had still drawn a blank. Who else? And then it came to her. The little gaoler at the prison had been friendly and helpful and, even though Bertha wasn't in his care, he might just come up with something. She bought a screwtop bottle of red wine at the Seaview and made her way to the minute prison. Samuel immediately invited her to sit on the bench outside and produced a flask of coffee.

"Can I tempt you?" he said.

"Unless you'd like something stronger," said Cissie, producing the bottle.

Samuel's face fell. "But I haven't got a corkscrew."

Cissie unscrewed the top and held the bottle up for inspection. "Chilean. Fourteen percent," was all she said.

Samuel took the bottle and filled two cardboard beakers with the welcome contents and then Cissie told him that he was her last chance. Samuel didn't say anything, but stood up, clasped his hands firmly behind his back and started to walk away. Then he disappeared from view, round one end of his small gaol. Cissie waited, and it was not long before the Malou gaoler reappeared, from round the other end of the Malou penitentiary, and resumed his seat.

"So?" said Cissie.

"You know Mortimer Trippe?"

"By reputation, yes. I've never met him."

Samuel nodded his head knowingly and looked up at Cissie, still saying nothing. And then Samuel shook his head knowingly, and again looked up. "I think I can guess what might have happened."

"What?" asked Cissie, wondering where this was all leading.

"When someone disappears on the Island, they're generally in this slammer, see?" He turned and gave the stonework an affectionate slap. "So if they're not here, where else could they be, I ask myself?" This was exactly what Cissie had spent hours asking *herself*, but she let Samuel continue. "I know this much," said the gaoler. "The Seigneur, fresh back from thirty or forty years' exile, is planning to knock this place down and build some modern thing to replace it." He paused. "Wanton destruction, if you ask me, but there it is. Anyway, someone goes missing now and isn't here? My bet is the Seigneur is somehow testing his new facilities on them. I don't know how."

"Well, I must say, Samuel, that does sound perfectly possible. But what am I supposed to do?"

"You can't do anything. Nor can anyone else on the Island. What you need is an Outsider, and one who has the necessary intro, if you see what I mean."

"Someone like Mortimer Trippe, you mean?"

"Not someone like him, Miss. Him. But one thing I think is necessary."

"Yes?"

"This matter is very – er, sensitive, as you might say."

"So?"

"He must come incognito."

"In disguise?"

"Essential. He's well known here, you see, and that counts against him."

"OK," said Cissie. If Mortimer Trippe was Hobson's Choice, disguised or not, so be it. She raised her glass. "Thank you, Samuel."

Samuel raised his glass too, and they both drank deeply.

* * *

As soon as Mortimer had woken up, early, thirsty and with a feeling of nervous malaise, after the terrible business with the tape-recorder, he had leapt out of bed and rushed downstairs still wearing his pyjamas, and a bright silk dressing-gown: all in the remote hope that he might have dreamt the part about wiping the recording clean, or that relative sobriety might produce a happier outcome. The Green Room was unlocked and the machine still on the mahogany table; try as he might, however, he had been unable to coax from it a single human sound.

In the equally forlorn hope that he might somehow get some sort of lead from the Sisterhood, he had stayed on at the White Lady (where he was now afforded every courtesy and comfort) for a couple of days. But, with their leader gone – and the private meeting irretrievably over – it became increasingly clear that Mortimer's continuing presence would achieve no more than had his presence in the past, and he had returned to London.

His homecoming was neither agreeable nor auspicious. Emily was waiting for him in the old-fashioned drawing-room of their South Kensington flat. The sun was streaming through the French windows of the first floor balcony, but its rays were not mirrored in Emily's glowering countenance. Sitting at a brass-topped trestle coffee-table, her appearance seemed to Mortimer to be reflected in the oil portraits hanging on every wall of Emily's fearsome-looking ancestresses, all resembling not only each other but also bearing a striking resemblance to their only living descendant. They appeared particularly fierce today – always a bad sign. Emily's lips were pursed and her arms tightly folded. She did not deign to look up as Mortimer came in. Rightly or wrongly, he decided on the light approach.

"Hello, old thing. How are things?"
Silence.

"Any news, so to speak?"

Emily pointed to the telephone. "Message," she grunted.

So that was it. A message on the answering machine must have upset her. But what could it possibly be? Mortimer would have preferred to listen to whatever it was in private, but they only had one telephone. He picked it up, dialled and listened. It was from someone called Cissie Sykes – whoever she might be – ringing from the Castle Hotel on Malou. The gist of her communication was that Mortimer should come with all haste to the Island as Lady Bertha was in urgent need of his presence. It was essential that he should come alone and effectively disguised. Well, it was a bit odd, certainly, but Mortimer still couldn't see why his wife seemed to be so upset.

"Thank you, Emily, I've deleted it. Er, was there anything else?"

"Only the matter of that piece in *High Society*."

"High society?" queried Mortimer, more puzzled than ever.

"You know perfectly well what I mean, Mortimer."

"Well, you might as well tell me in case it's slipped my mind," replied Mortimer, with a misjudged attempt at humour.

Emily waved a hand over the cutting from *High Society*, which lay on the table and which Annie Hoare had shown Emily in the Friar Tuck. Mortimer, who had not noticed it before, picked it up and examined it. He smiled reminiscently. "Oh that," he said. "It was Ladies' Day in the Seaview. The first they'd had there, actually with a new drink called Dames' Delight on offer. The ladies were naturally rather excited."

"So it would appear," said Emily sourly, "though for the life of me I am unable to understand why."

Mortimer knew from bitter experience that it would be best not to pursue the matter. "I think I'll just pop across the road, if you don't mind, Emily."

"To the Mockturtle Arms?"

"I thought so, yes."

"No doubt your system is crying out for alcohol."

"Yes," said Mortimer defiantly. "It is." He was also in strong need of a sympathetic male ear, and he knew that, as always at that time of day, his friend Adrian Darsham would be in the pub. He rose and headed for the door.

"I suppose you know it's only just turned eleven o'clock."

Mortimer, who had just arrived on the overnight train, did know and his pace increased.

Before her husband was even out of the door, Emily glanced at her watch; God, she was already late to meet Annie Hoare in the Friar Tuck.

* * *

In the absence of the Chief Sister at the White Lady Hotel a mood of extreme listlessness had overtaken the remaining members of the Sisterhood in their temporary island retreat. None had dressed at all formally on that cloudless morning; all lounged in beach clothes, of the requisite period, of course, on the luminous white beach, amidst a display of white and green – rugs, chairs, tables, parasols and liveried waiters flickering to and fro in the bright sun – everything resplendent against the backdrop of a silent sapphire sea. There the party had breakfasted simply off coffee and croissants, and now the first White Lady cocktails of the day were borne across the beach and set before them on spindly-legged beach-tables. This idyll would be disturbed only by the much-awaited news from far-off Malou. That would be the signal for departure from Radichsay, for the journey south, soon to be followed by the next, longer journey, to the Baltic and the capture of the prize. None doubted that the news would soon come.

But what was that? A disturbance in the waters of the bay. Hardly more than a few ripples, nothing so violent as a splash. A shoal of elegant white fish? A school of dolphins or porpoises? It was hard to say at that distance. Possibly, on this extraordinary island, some sort of nymphs down from the woods for their morning bathe. Or could they be the nuns from the Nunnery, reputed to bathe here, swimming out of their usual range for a closer look at the strange creatures on the hotel beach? Whatever they were, they soon swam away and the Sisters continued quietly to sip their White Ladies, while the waiters hovered in their striped tent, lest they should be needed for urgent replenishments.

But then more excitement. Every head turned as Mr Humphrey Bliss, proprietor and maître d'hôtel, tripped elegantly down the beach bearing a silver salver, on it a single envelope. The envelope, and indeed its contents, were already the talk of the Island, for receipt of a telegram was a rare event in this remote place. Humphrey lowered the tray so that Dr Mary Wildegoose could take from it both the envelope and the pearl-handled paper-knife which accompanied it.

The Deputy Chief Sister opened the envelope and quickly scanned the telegram. "A summons South," she said, and turned to Humphrey Bliss, indicating her glass. "Another round of these, I think, Mr Bliss, if you would be so kind. Am I right in thinking that there is a boat in the morning?"

"You are," said Humphrey and, with a nod at a waiter, withdrew.

Dr Mary then read the short missive out loud: "Lady Bertha unfortunately hospitalized. Return soonest. E.S."

CHAPTER 7

Old Colonel Hetherington was uncomfortably hot as he walked across the tarmac at Malou Airport. The recent cool spell had ended and the sun now blazed out of an azure sky, heightening the unsuitability in summer of a three-piece Harris tweed suit. Whether the plus-fours afforded more or less comfort the wearer was unable to decide but the knickerbocker suit was the only one which he had inherited from his Yorkshire grandfather Hetherington and at least it matched the rest of his appearance: a life-like grey wig, a now almost white moustache, a pair of steel-rimmed spectacles and a suitably lined and weathered face.

Mortimer had telephoned Cissie Sykes at the Castle Hotel once the flat was Emily-free after his return from the Mockturtle Arms and she had told him that Lady Bertha was being unlawfully held in Malou Castle. Since he was already 'on the case' and personally knew the Seigneur, he was the obvious candidate to come to the Island on the vital mission of mercy. Cissie had said that she had consulted the local gaoler, whom Mortimer would no doubt also remember, and he had strongly urged an effective disguise. This was essential, as well as was coming as soon as was humanly possible. She would not be at the airport to meet him as she was leaving the Island later that day. She would be sorry to miss him but wished him luck. Mortimer had decided to travel on his own passport, since the only person remotely likely to scrutinize it was Samuel, gaoler-cum-customs man, whose idea it had apparently been for him to travel incognito; it was unlikely in any case that they would even see each other since Samuel rarely troubled to exert himself by walking the short distance to the airport.

In this Mortimer was wrong, for the first person that he saw as he emerged from the airport building was his old friend the gaoler. Well, Samuel certainly wouldn't recognize him, so Mortimer decided to ignore him. Again he was wrong. As soon as Samuel saw the colonel he singled him out from the dozen or so arrivals and approached him with a broad smile. Good Lord, was his disguise so easily penetrated? Mortimer asked himself in alarm. Samuel was all nods and winks, accompanied by an embarrassingly grovelling obsequiousness. Not knowing what to say, Mortimer simply cringed and waited. With an imperious wave, the gaoler summoned the only pony and trap and told the driver to take 'the Colonel' to the Castle Hotel with all due speed. His old friend must have guessed the whole thing, right down to his rank and where he was staying! Finally Samuel lifted the colonel's suitcase onto the trap, smacked the pony quite unnecessarily on its rump and, with a cursory wave, strode purposefully back towards his diminutive prison-house.

As they set off, Mortimer was sure that the whole performance must have appeared thoroughly suspicious, but no one seemed to notice. He sat nervously on the edge of his seat, less confident now in the perfection of his appearance than he had been on arrival. Although he hoped not to have to spend a night on the Island, he had booked a room in the name of his long-dead grandfather, Colonel Hetherington, just in case, and at the hotel Barbara greeted him with due deference. She carried his suitcase up to his room, where he looked round appreciatively and said, "Thank you, my dear. Must just stretch the old pins before lunch, or rather before a quick pre-prandial snifter in the bar." He chortled, muttered that he would be back in half an hour or so and disappeared.

"What a dear old man," Barbara said to the waiter. "They don't make them like that any more."

"Thank God," said the waiter.

When Mortimer arrived at Malou Castle next door, he crossed the creaking drawbridge and pulled the old bell-chain. Angus the Scot opened the groaning oak door and asked if Mortimer was expected. Mortimer replied that he was not as he had been obliged to come as a matter of extreme urgency from London but that his name was Mortimer Trippe and he was well enough known to the Seigneur, as indeed he was throughout the Island. He continued by saying that he imagined that the Scot must be a recent Incomer. Angus nodded curtly and led Mortimer through to the presence; in the vaulted chamber the Scot waited by the door for instructions, while Mortimer greeted the Seigneur companionably. For a reply, he received a stony stare. Mortimer couldn't understand this at all.

"It's been a long time, Seigneur, must be all of a few weeks, but you do recognize me?"

The Lord of the Island turned to his attendant. "Wait there, Angus," he said and looked back at Mortimer. "I don't believe I've had the pleasure, Sir."

"But of course you know me. We met several times both before and after the trial. You must remember."

De Lessay looked back at the Scot. "Angus, if you would be so good." He nodded at the door.

And Mortimer was escorted from the premises.

Not until he was in the God-given fresh air did he realize his mistake. How could he have … he had forgotten to remove his disguise! Well, that was easily rectified. He repaired to his room in the hotel and, except for his natural and recent moustache, removed the facial disguise – using the aids with which his boss Mr Lamplighter had supplied him – and changed his clothes. Fine. Now he could go back to the Castle and this time … He didn't think that the wretched Scot had so much as passed his name on to the Seigneur, now he came to consider it, but of course even if he had, things would have been difficult to explain, to say the least. On reflection, it would probably be just as well if he hadn't; then he could simply go back as himself, so to speak and, apart perhaps from some initial difficulty with the Scot when he gave his name again, it should all be smooth sailing. Best probably not to go back too soon, though. Leave a decent interval or even the Seigneur might wonder what was going on. Just time for an unhurried drink in the bar, then he could start pretty well with a clean slate. But then Mortimer had the most appalling thought. He couldn't go to the bar without the disguise. He couldn't even go through the hotel without it but he couldn't go back to the Castle with it on. He was stuck. He sat on the bed with his head in his hands. There must be *something* he could do. Come on, Mortimer, you're a resourceful detective, you can't let a stupid thing like this have the better of you. And then, like a bolt from the heavens, it came to him. The fire-escape! As a result of various exigencies during the time that he had been employed in this hotel, he had perforce become familiar with the fire escape leading from his own room, as a means both of exit and re-entry and he could only hope that there was an equally convenient one from this room. He leapt to his feet and rushed to the window. Heaven be praised! There was one directly outside.

He changed quickly and in his eagerness forgot all about leaving a decent interval before returning to the Castle and climbed straight out, making sure that the window was firmly open for his return. So far as he could see there was no back way into the Castle, but the lane which ran almost past the bottom of the fire escape led by a devious route almost to the drawbridge. He would have to cover a bare fifteen yards of little-frequented open road before he was pretty nearly out of public view and almost at the Castle gate. Minutes later he was crossing the drawbridge, when he heard a shout from an upstairs window. He looked up and saw the Seigneur leaning menacingly out, wielding a shotgun. "Halt or I shoot."

"It's me," he called out. "Mortimer Trippe. I've come to visit you, Seigneur."

The feudal lord leaned further out and peered down. "Why, Mortimer!" he cried. "Come on in."

Once inside, the Scot gave Mortimer a very funny look, but said nothing and again showed him to the seigneurial chamber, in which they were joined by de Lessay himself. This time Mortimer was afforded a comfortable chair and a glass of whisky.

"Well, well, well," said Guy de Lessay. "Mortimer Trippe. Funny you coming so soon after the other fellow, barely half an hour ago. Talked complete gibberish and I'm pretty sure he was Hungarian, something like that. An interloper, of course. Armed, too, probably. Angus knew what to do with him, though."

"Scum," said the Scot, with a nasty look at Mortimer.

After this, Mortimer's business was soon transacted. When Guy de Lessay explained about Miss Sturdy's unexpected visit, Mortimer said that the woman was clearly an impostor. Without apparently doubting this assertion, de Lessay immediately became defensive. He said that he had smelt a rat about Elspeth Sturdy from the start, but hadn't been able to put a finger on his suspicions. Although he had known for some time that a visit from a Home Office official was impending, he had not expected this for at least another couple of weeks, and the woman with the admittedly strange letter had turned up so unexpectedly that he had been caught completely off guard. To be perfectly honest, he said, he had been more than a little preoccupied with his plans for very necessary and urgent penal reform on the Island and had at first misconstrued the purpose of the female's visit. He could see now that he had too readily consented to detain Lady Bertha Hook, and he clearly owed her ladyship an apology. The Seigneur added that, apart from these factors, he had had quite enough of Lady Bertha's constant and strident complaints and that the good Angus had made it clear in strong terms that he could endure the situation no longer.

If, therefore, Mortimer thought it desirable as a matter of justice, that her ladyship should be set free, he would be happy to oblige forthwith.

Mortimer thanked de Lessay for his help and said that he would be asking his friend Colonel Hetherington to return for Lady Bertha in half an hour, which should give her enough time to assemble her belongings and be ready to leave. He had to explain that the Colonel was in fact the man whom the Seigneur had earlier mistaken for a Hungarian and apologized profusely for the misunderstanding caused. It seemed that the Seigneur was so relieved at the turn of events that he had never troubled to ask Mortimer in what capacity he was rescuing the not-so-fair damsel in distress, nor did he enquire further about 'the Colonel'. Mortimer returned to his hotel room by the same clandestine route, regained his Colonel Blimp appearance, rang the airport, and went back to the Castle, where Lady Bertha was ready and waiting and seemingly no more anxious to make enquiries about her rescuer or his motives than had been the Seigneur. But there was bad news. Mortimer had learnt from the airport that fog was setting in and there would be no further flights in or out of the Island that day. He would have to spend the night in the hotel after all, and so would Lady Bertha.

As it was the waiter's evening off, Barbara was serving dinner and the presence of the old soldier and Lady Bertha at the same table struck a chord in her romantic heart. Mortimer had decided for a number of reasons not to disclose to Lady Bertha his true identity, not the least of which was to avoid any discussion about his recent visit to the island of Radichsay.

The old colonel and Lady Bertha were getting on well enough when something rather unfortunate occurred. When her ladyship mentioned that the only drink available in the Castle had been whisky, and that with meals she preferred wine, Mortimer, from force of long habit, rose from the table, went to the wine cupboard, took out a suitable bottle, uncorked it at the table and allowed Lady Bertha to taste it before pouring two glasses. He even had a napkin over his arm as he performed these functions. And then, before resuming his seat and again out of sheer habit, he picked up two empty dishes – and others from a nearby table – and took them to the serving hatch leading to the kitchen. When Barbara started to say that, grateful as she was for his help, it was really quite unnecessary, Mortimer suddenly realized what he had done.

"Oh, I say, Barbara, I'm frightfully sorry. I can't think what came over me," he said in his normal voice. Barbara gave him a funny look, as did her ladyship. And then, first with Barbara, the penny dropped.

"Mortimer!" she exclaimed in a voice for all to hear. "It's you."

The rest of dinner at Lady Bertha's table passed in a somewhat strained atmosphere. Mortimer himself was perforce circumspect in his account of the progress (or want of it) which he had so far made in his investigation: to the point, in fact, that her ladyship more than once lifted her eyes despairingly to the ceiling. For her part, she mentioned – as much, it seemed, for something to say as for any other reason – that the Sisterhood were largely parochial in the geographical scope of their activities and indeed had never operated outside the United Kingdom. Apart from Louise Loiseau (and leaving aside Mary Wildegoose's claimed knowledge of the ancient languages, including Sanskrit, and a number of obscure African dialects) none of the Sisters spoke any foreign language. All refused point-blank to travel by aeroplane. They were, said Lady Bertha, a curious bunch.

It hadn't been much to go on even combined with what other paltry information Mortimer had at his disposal but did this little all add up to some sort of pointer? Anyway, it was all he had, so one way or another he'd jolly well have to make the best of it. He'd better put on his thinking cap. And soon, for he sensed that there might not be a lot of time to play with.

* * *

The weather was hot in London as well. Somewhere east of the city, near Gravesend so far as it is possible to tell, stands the Thieves' Kitchen. It is an improbable pub in improbable surroundings – still so old-fashioned that it was perhaps more of a tavern than a public-house – encircled by an assortment of allotments and cabbage patches, derelict cottages and a working but far from prosperous farm. This hostelry nestles in a clump of trees on an island of near-countryside but with smoke-stacks and houses like dog-kennels clearly visible in the not far distance.

The building itself, of stone and slate, was formerly a farm and in its yard there still slink sheepdogs, getting under the feet of a donkey tethered to a post, with flies buzzing round its old head. At the front, in a small ill-tended patch of lawn, there is a beehive, but this does not deter the many customers, who leave their cars willy-nilly on whatever piece of rough ground looks free. The food, though basic, is excellent and the beer superb. Most Saturday afternoons they have jazz. It is Saturday now.

The four-piece band – trumpet, clarinet, trombone, upright piano – is warming up and a tall man with a beak of a nose is chatting to the audience about some of the jazz 'greats' – Sidney Bechet, Bix Beiderbecke, Django Reinhardt.

This is hardly a livelihood, but it should not be long before there will be no more passing the hat round for the Chamelions.

* * *

Lady Bertha – now for obvious reasons his real self, Bert – was rattled. As soon as he returned to London he asked Cissie Sykes to meet him in a boisterous Italian restaurant in Radnor Walk, off the King's Road, where the noise was likely to be such that they would not be overheard. As they sipped their

Campari sodas, Bert told his protégée of the extraordinary events involving Colonel Hetherington – aka Mr Mortimer Trippe – of the previous day. He said that he could make neither head nor tail of the man, whom after all he – she – had engaged as a private detective on a bloody important assignment. One moment the fucking man seemed to be a brilliant investigator – and he must have used considerable ingenuity in getting Lady Bertha out of clink – and the next a virtual cretin. Did Cissie have any views on the matter? Cissie did.

"Well, as a matter of fact, Bert, I had a bit of a chat with that sweetie Barbara at the hotel after you'd, er – disappeared. She said much the same thing."

"What exactly?"

"Well, she accepted that Trippe must somehow have been involved in solving the puzzle of that painting business – though she never quite understood how – but said that apart from that he as often as not behaved like a complete imbecile. The hotel manageress, though admittedly she was one of the conspirators, apparently said that Trippe was the stupidest man she had ever employed."

"Thanks, Cis. Not so good, eh?"

"Are you going to sack him then?"

"Christ, no. Couldn't risk it. He might be one of those buggers who are brilliant in their own field but plain crazy in every other way. His moronic behaviour could even be a cover, although from what I saw, I doubt it. Anyway, I've got to keep him on board."

"So?"

"It's quite simple. I need a second arrow in my quiver, some alternative, in case. And meanwhile I'm still under lock and key, remember. You haven't seen me."

CHAPTER 8

In the somewhat Spartan premises of the Four Eyes Private Enquiry Agency above a shoe shop in Kensington High Street, Mortimer was summing up as truthfully as was consistent with self-preservation – without stating anything that was actually untrue – the course of his investigation so far. Mr Lamplighter wore an expression of confused irritation. After a time, he looked at his watch and suggested that Mortimer should join him for luncheon at his club where, since a quiet corner could always be found even if the dining-room were crowded (it never was) they could continue their discussion undisturbed. As an afterthought he decided to invite Lionel too, his very useful personal assistant whom he invariably referred to as 'his clerk'. It was not unheard of, Mr Lamplighter said, only just outside Lionel's hearing, for 'his clerk' to come up with a useful idea. And so the three of them set off on foot for Kensington Square. The Young Professionals' Club was situated at the back of one of Kensington's grand houses, where it had had its premises for a very considerable time; some people found the name perplexing for Mr Lamplighter, a little older than Mortimer, was one of the youngest members and most of them had long since entered their sixth or seventh decades, as indeed had the only waiter, who was probably senior to them all. On arrival, Mr Lamplighter, like the busy professional man that he was, brushed aside a suggestion by a sort of porter in a dandruff-spattered black suit to go into the empty bar and made straight for the equally empty dining-room. Here, without consulting the others, he ordered three halves of keg beer, brown Windsor soup and boiled mutton, at which poor Lionel, who had been here before, gritted his teeth but said nothing. Only Mr Lamplighter seemed unaware that none of these substances had for decades been generally regarded with favour, except in a few old-fashioned establishments in the most far-flung outposts of the former British Empire. The host did, however, several times during the course of the meal, comment on the high quality of the fare; for dessert, again without so much as a glance at his guests, he ordered three peach Melbas. In the evening, he said, he quite often chose the treacle tart instead, but at luncheon, with an afternoon's brainwork still ahead, he found the peach Melba more readily digestible and, although he had never really had a sweet tooth, quite excellent. In the smoking-room afterwards (where smoking was now naturally not allowed) the host, in spite of his claim not to have a 'sweet tooth', called for three cherry brandies with their coffee.

"First class," pronounced Mr Lamplighter as he took a sip from the minute glass provided of the most saccharine beverage that Mortimer had ever tasted, or wished to taste. Before Mr Lamplighter's next utterance he looked round furtively to check that the room was empty: "Very well, back to business," he said, looking round the empty room with extreme caution. "It will take but little time to inform you, Lionel, of what few facts I myself and Mr Trippe know of this case." And he did so with admirable if inevitable brevity. "Now, Mr Trippe, is there anything else? I fear that I may have interrupted you when we were in the office."

There was little more to tell; in fact only what Lady Bertha had told Mortimer during their very unsatisfactory dinner together in the Castle Hotel on Malou. Mr Lamplighter sighed. "I see," he said "Well, the two matters for immediate discussion are, first, the probable location of the offence, and, secondly, its nature. Gentlemen?"

"I've already had a chance to give the first matter some thought," said Mortimer, moving aside with relief the small glass containing the poisonous substance of his host's choosing. He summed up the few facts to which they were all now privy, and continued. First Lady Bertha's wicked incarceration by Miss Sturdy prompted one or two tentative thoughts: it was clear from the very unhelpful tape-recording that the Sisters were keen that Lady Bertha should not be allowed to interfere with 'Phase Two of the Project' and the sudden action on Malou indicated a degree of urgency in this objective; also, they must have known that her ladyship could not be kept out of the way indefinitely, which indicated that a relatively short period of detention would suffice for their purpose, which in turn suggested that Lady Bertha would not be able to hinder their project after an initial, quite short period; and this could mean that by then they would need to be out of her reach, possibly out of the jurisdiction. Mortimer paused at this point but receiving no reaction from his audience, he ploughed on. Although this all pointed to the likelihood of whatever crime the Sisterhood was plotting being committed abroad, one had to bear in mind what Lady Bertha had explained was the apparently invariable geographically limited scope of the Sisterhood's activities. So abroad would probably not be too far abroad. Europe then? But with one exception they spoke no European languages and this would be a grave, possibly insuperable, impediment in the carrying out of a serious crime; certainly not one which they would take on voluntarily. So, was an English-speaking country to be their field of operation? But they also refused to fly. That meant travel by land or sea. And where in Europe could they go by road or rail, except to alien territory? What did that leave? Sea. A long sea voyage to America or some other English-speaking country seemed unlikely. So what else? A short sea voyage to somewhere not too far away?

That almost certainly meant a cruise, probably to the Mediterranean. And if the Sisters wanted to do their deed in a relatively familiar, English-speaking environment, where better than on a cruise liner? Mortimer looked at the two others in the still empty room for a reaction.

Lionel seemed as though he were about to speak, but was waved to silence by his master. Mr Lamplighter at first remained impassive but then clapped his hands delightedly and said, "Bravo! That is precisely the conclusion at which I had arrived myself. It is the only one, and I congratulate you on your analysis, Trippe. I always like to hear first from a subordinate, in case – as happens on rare occasions – he has got it right. You, I am glad to say, my dear Trippe, have. Although it is the inexorable conclusion, even I welcome a second opinion on matters as difficult as this. We think as one Trippe." He looked at Lionel. "And what do you think, Lionel?"

"I agree with Mr Trippe, sir."

"Right," said Mr Lamplighter, a little coolly, Mortimer thought, "We have the likely venue, at least in general terms. Now we must consider the nature of the intended crime."

They did, and it did not prove as difficult as Mortimer had imaged. For a start, several types of offence could be eliminated on the basis of motive alone. A bunch of mostly middle-aged women (and the 'Honorary Woman') would have no reason to commit a terrorist act, for example. Indeed anything without a financial motive could almost certainly be excluded, so out almost certainly went any sort of murder or arson without a financial motive. What did that leave? Fraud, theft, kidnap, extortion – there wasn't much else, at least that any of them could think of. Fraud on a holiday cruise ship? Hardly even a runner. Theft? It was possible. Mr Lamplighter had once been on a cruise liner, many years ago, and he said that there had been a painting exhibition and also jewellery for sale, but doubted whether a prospective criminal would know this in advance; even if they did, the practical difficulties of stealing paintings on a ship could rule that out and some sort of smash and grab seemed equally improbable, not least because of the problem of disposing of the booty. Kidnap? Kidnap? Er – yes, kidnap had to be counted as a distinct possibility: no doubt plenty of rich people on board and it would have the additional advantage, from the point of view of the criminal, that the takings could be extorted gradually after the event, without the need for ready cash on board; a kidnap would presumably have to be effected in port and the kidnappers then disappear, but that would not be insuperable at all. Extortion? See under kidnap, said Mr Lamplighter.

So, thought Mortimer, it looked like kidnap on a cruise-liner.

On the way back to the office, Lionel said something which struck Mortimer as odd. "Do you know something, Mr Trippe?" He nodded towards Mr Lamplighter. "He is one of that rare breed – nearly all men – who have a first-class brain behind an air of complete other-worldliness. Just look at him now," he added, as Mr Lamplighter nearly stepped under the wheels of a lorry and, for the second time that day, had to be hauled to safety by 'his clerk' tugging at his coat-tails. "Perhaps that's why you and he think so much alike." Mortimer made no reply to this observation but pondered it for some time in continuing bafflement.

* * *

Mr Lamplighter lost no time in setting in motion his plans to ascertain as much as was necessary to enable Mortimer to join whatever cruise it was likely to be. In order to make a reservation he knew from Lionel's general enquiries that it was necessary to do so well in advance, at least to obtain a relatively comfortable stateroom, although a humble cabin, probably shared, could on most lines be obtained at the last minute, even if it were in the bowels of the ship, with no view whatever and the sound of the engines to be endured instead of the soothing sounds of the sea to be savoured. Even so humble a berth could obviously not be obtained without knowing the port and line and name of the ship and the date of sailing. Mr Lamplighter was sure that the departure would be from a UK port, and since all the group lived in London, this almost certainly meant Harwich, Dover or Southampton. Mr Lamplighter would have one of the group tailed to find out which, and if, as seemed likely, they were travelling to the port by train, this could be ascertained from the London station used; if they travelled by road they could be discreetly followed from Central London until the destination was obvious. With the date, port and an approximate time the name of the ship could then be deduced for, if it were a two-week cruise, the destination would probably be the Mediterranean or the Baltic, if three weeks, then a little further afield, but in no case would more than one cruise be leaving from the same port at more or less the same time to any of the possible destinations. Whatever the case, however, no arrangements could be put in hand until the last minute. For the group member to be tailed Mr Lamplighter had unhesitatingly selected Mr Cyril Jinks; he lived not far away at World's End and was noticeably large with an idiosyncratic appearance and gait. Mr Lamplighter had a watch kept on his address and had given instructions for him to be tailed whenever he went out.

* * *

Two days later Mr Lamplighter received a call from his man tailing Jinks. He was at Victoria Station with a large suitcase. This, Mr Lamplighter deduced, meant that the ship would be sailing from Dover that day, probably in the late afternoon. Lionel then worked out, with the help of a few telephone calls, that the vessel was the Lucky Lady of the Liberian Luxury Lines and that its destination was the Baltic. He reserved Mortimer a cabin, not by any means the best, but

69

managed to talk briefly to the purser who intimated, with a conspiratorial chuckle, that in certain special circumstances an upgrade might be possible. Mr Trippe should in any event now leave for Dover as soon as possible.

CHAPTER 9

At Dover Mortimer took a taxi from the station to the docks.

"The Lucky Lady, sir? Can't say I've heard of her, but I'll give it a go."

At the prescribed dock and quay, Mortimer, much to his consternation, saw only a vessel of the most monstrous proportions; it looked to be the height of St Paul's Cathedral and in length must have extended to hundreds of yards. Mortimer had heard of these mega cruise liners; they contained endless acres of the most horrendous kinds of entertainment, to which their mostly youthful passengers were constantly urged by strident tannoy messages; worse, they held about four thousand people, including crew. How on earth, Mortimer wondered, could he ever hope to find his kidnap target and the kidnappers in such a colossus? A needle in a haystack would hardly be more difficult to detect.

"That *could* be her," the driver said doubtfully as he dropped Mortimer off, pointing to a much smaller and humbler vessel moored almost beneath the bows of its gigantic neighbour and which in comparison looked almost like a tug. "And good luck to all who sail in her," the taxi-man added with a laugh.

Despite these ominous words Mortimer felt encouraged. This – and it was indeed the Lucky Lady – was much more to his taste. Whether it was of pre- or post-war construction he neither knew or cared, and he remembered now the description in the brochure which Lionel had shown him: 'A ship for the discerning passenger. The best of the old, the best of the new. Deck-games, not dance-halls, and definitely no theatre, ice-rinks or bowling-alleys. Good food in preference to a dozen fancy restaurants. Commanded by the best Greek officers on the seas and staffed with all the courtesy and efficiency of both East and West. Old time romance AND all modern conveniences, with the *very latest in security*. The perfect choice.' Mortimer decided to go aboard.

As he started to make his way to the gangway, however, he found himself blocked by both uniformed guards and ropes; he was directed to a low oblong wooden building with a corrugated iron room which had about it the look of a small transit billet for refugees or even a disinfecting shed for animals. Inside, three cheerful middle-aged women sat at small desks beside turnstiles, outside which were queues of expectant looking passengers, all talking excitedly. Mortimer was shown to the longest queue and waited his turn. When it came, the woman at the desk – perhaps on account of Mortimer's less than jolly demeanour – lost her cheerful look and at once assumed the stern mask of officialdom. First, she asked if he was travelling alone; then, while looking at his passport, she wished to know his name, address, date and place of birth, mother's maiden name, his profession and 'purpose of travel'. Mortimer was not prepared for the last two questions, and it must have showed.

"Well, I used to be a chartered accountant, you know."

"*Used* to be?"

"Yes." He paused. "I still am, actually."

"But you just said you *used* to be."

"And I also said that I still am."

The woman pressed a red button on her computer and typed in a few words.

"And your purpose of travel?"

"Pleasure," said Mortimer unhesitatingly, but looking as he said it the complete antithesis of a happy holiday-maker.

"Really?" The surprise was not even thinly disguised. "And you are alone?"

Mortimer said nothing and the woman pressed the red button again and typed something more into her machine. "This is your pass, Mr Trippe," she said finally, handing Mortimer a small object the shape and size of a credit card. "It is twofold in purpose. It is both the key to your stateroom and, more importantly, your SeaPass card for going ashore and returning to the ship."

"Thank you."

"You may go aboard now." This intimidating female looked Mortimer directly in the eye. "But report at once to the purser."

"Where is ..." Mortimer began, but he was propelled through the turnstile by a male security guard before he could finish. He had little difficulty in finding the purser's office, on Deck 1, but why on earth was he wanted? The security woman had clearly believed neither his profession nor the purpose of his travel. But what powers did a purser have? Mortimer knew that in former days they were naval paymasters, but what was their function now?

The purser proved to be a friendly, even ingratiating man, of swarthy appearance, who spoke a very peculiar sort of American English. But when Mortimer gave his name the man immediately looked businesslike.

"Your SeaPass please, Mr Trippe."

Mortimer handed the card over and the purser inserted it in some mysterious looking machine and waited for it to reappear. "I see. Well I don't figure you'll be *there* for long."

"Where?" The purser ignored him. Was he to be thrown off the ship as soon as he had been allowed onto it, however grudgingly; and just as he had made at least *some* headway in his assignment for Lady Bertha? He waited.

"I guess a move is indicated," continued the purser, "right now. What do *you* think, Mr Trippe?"

"Well I don't know, really, you know. I'm new to all this."

"Deck Zero, eh? Down near the bowels of the ship. And remote, too."

Did they want him in a more prominent position, so they could keep an eye on him? Mortimer wondered. Well, Deck Zero was better than being chucked off completely, he supposed, but he didn't like the purser's tone. "It sounds fine," he said.

"Fine? No view, a sonovabitch of an attendant shared with a dozen other crap-holes? Is that what you call fine? It's one of the most god-awful berths on board."

"Well, I do like a bit of peace and quiet," Mortimer said cagily.

"Peace and quiet!" the man almost shouted. "You gotta be jokin'. Room 1, Deck Zero's as near as dammit in the goddam engine room. Gee, you got funny taste, mister." He produced two large photographs and handed them to Mortimer with a shrug.

The first was of a cramped, windowless cabin, empty except for a bunk-bed, an upright chair and a small table; the second photograph appeared to show a luxury hotel bedroom, not only beautifully furnished but with a wide balcony from which as a backdrop was visible a stunning sunset – a 'stateroom' if ever there was one, thought Mortimer. "You pays your money," said the purser with a smirk, "and you takes your choice."

It was at this point that Mortimer remembered what Lionel had told him about the possibility of an upgrade. Nothing questionable, just a straightforward business transaction. He pulled out a wad of US dollar bills, the currency used on the Lucky Lady.

"Not so fast," said the purser. "Have you handed in your credit card at Reception yet?"

"No, I was told to come straight here."

"OK, give it to me."

Having not yet agreed a price for the transaction, Mortimer was cautious. "But –"

"I ain't gonna take nothing off it. That comes later. We're a strictly no-cash ship. Sign for everything. Live now, pay later, you might say." And he emitted what sounded like a rather nasty chuckle, but Mortimer handed his card over and the purser placed it in a metal box and gave Mortimer a piece of paper. "Now, that stateroom. You want an upgrade, right?"

"How much would it be?"

"Fifteen hundred bucks to you, Mr Trippe."

Well, thought Mortimer, Lady Bertha was footing his expenses, so why not?

"Very well, put it on my account."

"Cash," said the purser.

"But you just said everything was strictly no-cash."

"This is different," the man said with an unmistakable wink.

"Do I get a receipt?"

" 'Course you get a receipt. I'll make it out for cash received for car-hire arranged in various ports. OK?"

Meekly, Mortimer who, in ignorance of the no-cash rule, had obtained a fistful of dollars before leaving London, handed over the sum demanded.

His stateroom – did that sound too pompous or should he call it simply a room, or a cabin or what? – was on Deck 4, just below the uppermost deck, the Promenade Deck. He managed to open the door with the SeaPass card at the fourth attempt. And he had to admit that the room was all that the purser had hinted; well worth seven or eight hundred pounds of Lady Bertha Hook's money. Exhausted by the various hazards that he had so far encountered, however, Mortimer decided that before doing anything else he would have a nap, and prostrated himself on the huge and very comfortable bed. Sleep came quickly. But so did a sudden awakening.

There was a tap at the door and a man of barely five feet in height, of Asiatic appearance and wearing a smart white uniform, presented himself.

"Good afternoon, sir. I am Ramon, your stateroom attendant. I shall be looking after your needs throughout the voyage."

"Oh, er, that's very kind of you. Just having a bit of a nap, I'm afraid."

"Excellent, excellent. Shall I unpack your belongings, sir?"

"Er, later, or rather thanks but I'll do that myself. Very kind of you, all the same."

"Excellent idea. Is there anything I can get you, sir?"

"No thank you very much. I think I'll just continue my nap for a bit, if that's all right."

"Excellent plan, Mr Mortimer," said Ramon, and withdrew.

Sleep came less easily this time and almost as soon as it did – or so it seemed – Mortimer was once more wakened. He became drowsily aware of another, far less benign, presence. On his so far unexplored balcony loomed the tall, shadowy figure of a man. Mortimer tried to tell himself that he was dreaming, but he did not believe it himself. He rubbed his eyes and blinked. The unwanted apparition was still there. So he *was* being spied on. He sat up.

But then the intruder spoke: "Hope I didn't disturb you, old man. Just inspecting our quarters, you see."

Not a spy, obviously, but who the Dickens could he be? A madman of some sort? A stowaway?

If ever a man deserved a very direct rebuff this one did, but Mortimer, still only half-awake, found himself adopting a quite different approach.

"Don't worry about me," he said. "Feel free, as they say."

"That's very civil of you," the man said, stepping inside and looking round appreciatively. "You seem to have drawn the long straw, if I may say so."

"What on earth do you mean?" said Mortimer, realizing that the chap was impervious to irony and struggling up from the bed.

"Well, all this is really a suite, as you can see," said the other, indicating a long and now closed off connecting partition between the two rooms. "Yours is obviously the sitting-room with a bed shoved in. My part's a bit cramped, to be honest, though I don't suppose I should complain in the circumstances."

"What circumstances?" asked Mortimer, now with a faint glimmering of understanding; and then feeling that the barest requirements of hospitality called for an introduction, said who he was, to which the 'guest' replied in kind: Jamie Scott-Munro.

"Anyway the upgrade, Mortimer – I think as room-mates we can use first names – not at all bad, as upgrades go. Four real roughnecks had booked in here and Ramon wouldn't have it. So they did a swap. The louts to the dungeons, the gents up here. Rather satisfactory, when you think about it."

Mortimer's understanding increased, if only marginally.

Jamie elaborated. Ramon hadn't been happy with the situation up here and he, Jamie, had been far from happy with his quarters below and had tackled the purser about it. The whole situation was screaming out for a fair exchange, but who else was to come up here? And then the purser had remembered that there'd been another tentative request for an upgrade from the dungeons, and had told security to alert the man involved. Security had realized that this other man, whatever else he might be, was at least a gent and bingo, that was it, here they were and it hadn't cost a brass farthing. But when Mortimer explained that he himself had paid a considerable sum for the exchange, Jamie laughed sympathetically.

"Rough with the smooth, old man. You win some, you lose some. Thanks anyway, very decent of you, even if the purser did trouser the proceeds. All's well that ends well." Suddenly his eyes became transfixed. "God, that looks like a mini-bar. I'd been wondering about that. Saves tipping Ramon every time you want a snort. Should have thought of that. Now I come to think of it it's obvious they'd put it in the reception room. What'll you have, Mortimer?"

"Well I don't think I've had any lunch yet. Isn't it getting a bit late?"

"Ring for something, old man. Twenty-four hour service, you know. Drink first. Bad for you not to settle the nerves on arrival."

This was enough for Mortimer, and he nodded. Without another word Jamie opened the small walnut cabinet containing Mortimer's mini-bar and poured them each two 'miniature' bottles of whisky. Then, settling back in the most comfortable chair, he crossed his long legs and lit an illicit cigarette.

"Life on the ocean wave," he sighed happily, gazing out over the tranquil water of Dover.

* * *

On a fine weekday morning, shortly before noon, Bert Pyman (frequently and for excellent reasons known as Lady Bertha Hook) and Cissie Sykes were sitting in a shady part of the garden of the Windsor Castle pub in Campden Hill Road. Bert had in front of him a pint of beer while Cissie was sipping a glass of white wine. An onlooker – though the garden was now quiet and the few other customers preoccupied with each other – might have taken them for father and daughter; a self-made rough diamond, perhaps, with an expensively but badly educated daughter; or possibly, to anyone who knew Cissie, something less conventional, for it was known that the young lady had catholic tastes in men, often running to a disparity in age or class, or both.

"I don't think I told you, Cis, but Trippe rang me at my new address before he left."

"Left? Where's he gone?"

"He's gone on a Baltic cruise. He's worked out that that's where my dear Sisters are operating and he's almost sure it's going to be a snatch."

"A snatch?"

"Kidnap. He doesn't know who of or who by but it seems to make sense. I just hope to Christ he's not having one of his mad-bad spells."

"Jesus! And what about – what was it – the other arrow in your quiver?"

"All sorted, Cis. They're on board too."

"On board."

"In both senses. In my employment and on the ship. Four o' the bastards."

"Now you tell me. When did all this happen?"

"Coupla days back. Couldn't get hold of you, could I?"

"So?"

"So I've hired the Sink Street Mob to carry out a pre-emptive strike."

"Christ! And am I supposed to know of this Sink Street lot?"

"You might have, you might not have. I did, obviously. Nasty bunch. Four o' the worst in fact. Not what you'd call good-looking either but not as dumb as they seem."

"Thugs, then?"

" 'Course they're thugs, sweetheart. What else? But clever thugs, an' they'll need to be."

"You mean they've got to work out who the target is?"

"Well, Cis, they can hardly snatch the fucking target if they don't know who the fucker is, can they? An' they may need to figure out who the other lot are too, whoever the Sisters have hired."

"To knock them off?"

"Nah. Too dangerous. Just to stay one jump ahead, Cis."

"And how much did you have to fork out for these stinkers?"

"None of your bloody business, but this type doesn't come cheap."

"And you got them through Mr Thirty Per Cent?"

"Obviously. And he insisted they had the best accommodation still available on the ship. There was only a suite left and on the best deck, so they're in there."

"Won't they – er – stand out a bit?"

"A bit? Three of the four with shaven heads and the other one with dreadlocks. Yes, they will a bit, but I paid well over the odds. Arm and a fucking leg, in fact."

"Dreadlocks? Is one of them black then?"

"Yellow," said Bert gloomily. "Or red, I forget which. But the agent says they know how to behave when they want to and they've got all the gear – black tie and that."

* * *

On his way to dinner that evening Mortimer, wearing a dinner jacket which was more or less a family heirloom but, at a slight pinch, still fitted him, stopped for refreshment at the Lucky Lady's Champagne Bar. This agreeable pre-dinner venue sold little champagne (unsurprisingly at a hundred dollars a bottle for the ship's own brand) but it provided entertainment in the form of a musical quintet billed as 'The Chameleons'. This consisted of Mart Rüütel (Vocalist and widely known as 'the Beak'), Edgar Laar (Violin), Andres Vähi (Cello), Manish Lahiri (Bass) and Natalia Tarand (Piano). The musicians played while Mart Rüütel, a tall man with a prodigious nose, occasionally sang the sort of tunes which Mortimer had hoped and expected to hear in these surroundings, mostly romantic numbers from the 1930s and 1940s. The audience, too, was much as he had expected, consisting for the most part of middle-aged and elderly British and Americans. Unlike many cruise liners, where the dress requirements for dinner vary from 'smart-casual' (which would, of course, have baffled Mortimer) to formal, the Lucky Lady insisted every evening on black tie for gentlemen and equivalent attire for ladies, and everyone appeared to have complied.

In one corner, deep in conversation with and obviously charming two elegant young women, was Jamie Scott-Munro, Mortimer's unexpected room-mate. Faultlessly dinner-suited, Jamie now presented a considerably more impressive appearance than had been the case during their curious encounter of the afternoon. His dishevelled thick black hair was greying at the sides, his weather-beaten countenance and rough, regular features those of an old-style adventurer. A bottle of champagne in an ice-bucket stood on his table.

In this agreeable if unexciting atmosphere Mortimer's enjoyment of the music was punctuated with less pleasant thoughts of what lay in store. He had never in his life felt quite so conspicuously alone and the more he thought about his mission the more insuperable the obstacles seemed: he was still in little doubt that the Sisterhood were planning a kidnap during the voyage – probably in one of the half dozen or so Baltic ports – but with well over a hundred people on board and no discernible clues he had little enough to go on. Jamie himself was obviously something of a loose cannon but who else among this polite and well-groomed throng could be either perpetrators or victim? The Sisters themselves would presumably be on board in some sort of supervisory or monitoring role, but they would obviously not be likely to give much away. As Mortimer looked round to catch a waiter's eye, however, the almost seamless gentility was seriously vitiated by the entry into the Champagne Bar of four gentlemen of a very different stamp.

Two were tall and two were short, the tall ones lean and hungry in appearance, the short ones built, it seemed to Mortimer, like rugby prop-forwards. Three chose to wear no head hair at all whilst the fourth, though, whatever else, was by no means African-featured, wore Rastafarian dreadlocks. In compliance with the ship's dress code all wore black bow ties, but of hugely varying shapes and sizes, together with frilly-fronted white shirts and wing collars. But their 'dinner jackets', variously plain, spotted and striped, omitted few of the colours of the spectrum. Sitting down, they too ordered champagne, but Dom Perignon in preference to the house-brand.

At the entry of these peacocks, the Chamelions had briefly stopped playing and there were nods and whispers round the bar.

What on earth was he to make of this? Mortimer wondered as he rose to go into dinner – with the prospect of a sea of scores of unknown faces – quite alone?.

CHAPTER 10

The dining-room was nearly full by the time that Mortimer got there, so it seemed that the drinkers in the Champagne Bar must all be late birds. He was shown to one of the far corners, which gave him the chance to look at his fellow passengers on his way through the room. They were a more assorted lot than those (save the mostly criminal-looking characters who had ordered Dom Perignon) sipping their drinks to the sound of the Chamelions, some of the men even in lounge suits and a greater number of exotic-looking foreigners than Mortimer had expected, including a sprinkling of well-dressed and fastidious-looking black people of, it seemed from their accents, both American and African provenance. There were also a number of children sitting politely with their prosperous-looking parents, which immediately put Mortimer in mind of lopped off fingers and ears posted mysteriously in buff envelopes.

Initially relieved to be seated at a table on his own, but soon again self-conscious about his obvious conspicuousness, he studied the menu, deciding that Lady Bertha had not done him at all badly. All food – though not drink – was included in the overall cost of the cruise, although a few of the swankier items had an asterisk beside them denoting 'supplementary charge' without specifying the amount. Mortimer chose two of these dishes – oysters and crayfish – and ordered half a bottle of Muscadet-sur-Lie. Hardly had the dozen oysters been placed before him than he heard a familiar voice.

"Mind if I join you, old boy?"

Without waiting for a reply Jamie sat down on the chair pulled back for him by a waiter, glanced unenthusiastically at the menu and ordered soup and cutlets. When asked what he would like to drink, he said, 'Tap water with no ice' and looked enviously, it seemed to Mortimer, at the oysters. Silence ensued.

"What happened to your lady friends?" Mortimer enquired eventually.

"Lady friends? Oh them – dead loss. Cost me a small fortune. They never even offered, and rich as Croesus, by the look of them."

"Have a glass of wine," Mortimer said encouragingly, holding out his bottle.

Jamie brightened. "That's very kind of you, Mortimer. But it's on the strict understanding that I can't …"

"Don't worry, that's all right. I'll get another bottle."

Jamie looked at him sharply. "You on expenses?"

"No. I wish I – . Well, partly, if you see what I mean."

"I don't, actually, but never mind," said Jamie, taking a sip of the wine. "Bit of a rum old tub, this." He looked round the room, at the artificial portholes and nautical artefacts festooning the walls. "I'm going to have my work cut out, by the look of it." And with this enigmatic remark he devoted his attention to his soup, with only occasional glances at Mortimer's dwindling dozen *fines de claire*.

Jamie then continued disconsolately, almost as though talking to himself. "With women clearly not a runner – I must be getting too old, if you want the honest truth – I'll have to turn my hand to something else."

"Oh, er – will you?"

"Obviously. I've got to do something, whether I like it or not. See those Sink Street johnnies in the bar, by the way? They've just come in here."

"Those what?"

"The hoods. The pretty boys. With that lot around someone's sure to need personal security. Question is, who?"

"I'm afraid I don't quite follow."

"Well," Jamie looked round cautiously, "you know, sort of bodyguard stuff. Can't say I like it, but it wouldn't be the first time. Not as tricky as it sounds, actually, when you get the hang of it. More brain than brawn, in fact, but not for beginners. Obviously."

Mortimer was interested. "You mean you'd actually work as a bodyguard for someone?"

"Be glad to. Might be nothing else for it. Problem is, who needs one?"

"So what d'you think these Sink Street fellows are up to?"

"Remains to be seen," said Jamie, "but they're not here for the sea air, believe me."

At this point, the last diners to come in, all five of the Sisterhood – dressed to the nines – strode majestically to the centre of the room where, surrounded by clucking waiters, they graciously took their seats.

The Lucky Lady was now well out of sight of land and on course for the North Sea.

* * *

Lady Bertha Hook was happily ensconced deep within the tasteful surroundings of her Mayfair club. The downstairs bar, with its chandeliers, elaborately moulded ceiling and walls, and Chippendale furniture was unlike any other bar in London; it had, in fact, more the aura of a grand 18th century drawing-room than of a drinks dispensary, and Lady Bertha felt very much at home there. She had recently – if reluctantly – concluded that the uncouth Bert Pyman was by no means always for her; for much of the time she now preferred her adopted self, the forceful daughter of a long-dead and somewhat murky earl. And in her club she was accorded the deference rightfully belonging to a person of her supposed rank.

Bertha now had to admit that there was something darker in her preference. Not only had she become a snob, and derived considerable pleasure from the subterfuge, with its risks and unaccustomed reactions from others, but she found, oddly enough, that her new persona enhanced more than a little her relationship with the delectable Cissie. Even to herself she dwelt as little as possible on this aspect of the matter, but that it existed was as incontestable as her title was not. She was waiting for Cissie now, safe in the knowledge that the Sisters would be well out at sea and that none of their, or for that matter Bert Pitman's associates, would ever penetrate her Mayfair redoubt.

Why could the wretched girl never be on time? Lady Bertha wondered irritably. Perhaps she thought that being late was the prerogative of her class; perhaps, it suddenly struck her ladyship with the force of a blow, Cissie did not consider her, as one of the lower orders, worthy of punctuality. Such an idea was not to be endured. Bertha had adopted her masquerade with such enthusiasm and assiduousness that she now found it easier to fall into the part of Bertha than she did to fall out of it and to revert to the plebeian Bert, whom she was even beginning a little to despise. Lady Bertha's mode of speech, her accent and haughty manner – all came to her now as readily as breathing. If Cissie thought for one moment … but here she was now, looking, Bertha had to admit, in the appalling parlance of the cinema-goer, like a million dollars.

"Bit like a morgue in here," commented Cissie, as she sat down, and in a voice which must easily have pierced even the torpor of Lady Bertha's fellow members.

"Large gin and tonic please," Cissie said to the waiter without a flicker of acknowledgement of the man's presence.

"They only serve large ones here," Bertha said crushingly.

"Well that's what I asked for, isn't it?"

"Alright, alright. Anyway, Cissie, I need your help."

Cissie looked pleased. "Anything for you, my lady."

God, thought Bertha, don't say she's in one of her piss-taking moods. But there were other members too close to remonstrate, for it couldn't be assumed that virtual deafness was universal in the Mayfair Ladies' Club. "You once went on a cruise, didn't you, Cissie?"

"Yeah. Average age about the same as here. Not bad all the same."

"Good. Now what I want to know is the procedure for joining the ship in mid-voyage."

Cissie looked at her ladyship in astonishment. "You're not intending to join this cruise yourself, are you?"

"And may I ask why not?"

"It'll be tricky. Tight security these days. You can't get on the thing at will wherever it happens to stop. It's not like a train."

And Cissie explained the procedure, at least that which had obtained on her ship, which she assumed would be pretty much the same on any cruise. You were given a pass which had to be plugged into a computer whenever you went ashore and ditto on the way back. Each pass was personal and couldn't be switched. She didn't remember them photographing you, as the pass was all they needed. It was foolproof. If you had a pass you got off and if you had a pass you could get back on again. If not, not. It was as simple as that. The only other way, if there was still room, to join the thing in the middle would involve complex booking and security arrangements, if it was possible at all, which Cissie doubted. Bertha would have to forget it.

But Bertha wouldn't forget it. "Surely someone in my position … A title even in these days must count …"

"Not a chance, Bertha. And even if you *did* manage to get on, and it's a damn big if, you wouldn't be able to go as Lady Bertha Hook, or Mr Bert Pyman or Mr Tom Cobley for that matter. You'd have to take pot luck."

"Pot luck?"

"Run of the cards. Whatever name comes up. Might not even be able to choose your sex. You might just as easily end up Mr Smith as Mrs Jones. All depends."

"Whatever *are* you talking about, girl? Depends on what?"

"Whose boarding pass you could nick. Or, more likely, *I* could nick. It's as simple as that, Bertha.

* * *

"Fancy a nightcap in the Piano Bar after dinner, Mortimer? First one's on me."

Mortimer agreed, though not doubting whom subsequent 'nightcaps' would be on.

The Chamelions were once more providing the entertainment, although now with muted saxophone and trumpet instead of strings, as well as background percussion and a later evening repertoire; also with the Beak now on piano and the girl crooning; perhaps their versatility gave rise to their name, Mortimer thought. When, inevitably, Mortimer and Jamie's conversation turned to their normal lives, Jamie remained enigmatic but managed to give the impression that, as Mortimer was now beginning to suspect, he lived largely on his wits. He himself explained that he was an accountant, even if something of a square peg in a round hole; he continued by explaining that as a result of marital difficulties with a much loved wife he had come near to a nervous collapse and his employers had sent him on this trip, all reasonable expenses paid, for the sole purpose of recuperation in order that he might return to London a new man and participate more happily and profitably in the activities of the firm. Jamie's only interruption to the easy flow of this vile fabrication was at the words 'all reasonable expenses paid', when he turned and asked if the waiter would be good enough to spare them a moment. As he turned, however, he saw not merely the waiter but all five members of the Sisterhood who had, with one exception, just taken their seats in, as usual, the most prominent position.

Cyril Jinks, tiring no doubt of being obliged as usual to listen to female clacking, had chosen not to sit down but to approach the bar where he chose to engage the barman in some alternative conversation. Elspeth Sturdy and Dr Mary Wildegoose were talking in low voices between themselves, whilst the two more engaging in appearance of the ladies, Gloria Ollerenshaw and Louise Loiseau, looked around the bar with some alertness, occasionally exchanging remarks. It was upon these two that Jamie fixed a professional eye.

"What do you think, Mortimer?" he asked, nodding in the direction of these two.

"Oh, er, yes. An unusual looking group," Mortimer muttered non-committally.

"I'll ask them over," said Jamie. "You never know." And without another word he was on his feet. Mortimer saw the well practised look of charm, the flattered reaction and heard the words, "… join my friend and me for a glass of something." And in the blink of an eye Mortimer found himself sitting in by no means disagreeable proximity to the comely Frenchwoman whilst her Yorkshire sister-in-crime was looking appreciatively into the guileless grey eyes of the seasoned adventurer. Mortimer talked enthusiastically of France and matters French to Madame Loiseau, whilst Jamie was no doubt regaling the lovely black Gloria with tales of a lifetime's exploits in situations more thrilling than they were probable. Drinks arrived, and more drinks, and Mortimer could see Lady Bertha's expenses tally mounting by the moment. And then Gloria Ollerenshaw suddenly turned to him.

"Excuse me, Mr Trippe, but don't I know you?"

Mortimer went cold. "No, no. Not at all. I'm quite sure we've never met. In fact I wouldn't recognize you even on a desert island."

"Funny you should say that –"Gloria cut herself short. "Sorry. Must be mistaken." Even as she spoke a piercing female voice with an artificially posh accent broke in on the proceedings.

"Why, if it isn't Mortimer Trippe. Fancy seeing you here."

Mortimer's look of curiosity quickly turned to one of horror. Gloria Ollerenshaw nudged Louise Loiseau. "Well, we won't intrude. You seem to be well known around here, Mr Trippe," she said, standing up. "I do hope we shall meet again, Mr Scott-Munro. Goodnight everyone."

Jamie rose, elaborately kissed both Gloria and Louise on the hand and bowed and the Sisters went back to their party. Mortimer spluttered his good-byes and turned back to this fresh threat to his peace of mind and her quietly smiling consort.

The woman sat down in Gloria's vacated seat and, after a brief hesitation, her husband sat down too. Mortimer remembered them all too well from his job as a tour guide with the dreadful Eurolux Tours, which he had taken in desperation after his sacking two years ago from the firm of chartered accountants by which he had been employed for most of his working life.

"Hello, Mrs Fox-Vasey. I'm equally surprised to see you. Good evening, Major," he said to her husband, for whom his main feeling had always been one of pity. During the European coach tour this ghastly woman had been nothing but a menace, and Mortimer sensed trouble now. He glanced uneasily at Jamie and in doing so saw Gloria whispering to Miss Sturdy and Dr Wildegoose and looking meaningfully in his direction. While Ursula Fox-Vasey, to the accompaniment of bored but obedient nods from her long-suffering husband George, was repeatedly assuring Mortimer – as she had done so many times during the course of the ill-fated Eurolux tour – that, having suffered such trauma at the hands of Eurolux, she would never risk a coach tour again. Mortimer saw Mary

Wildegoose twice approach the Beak of the Chamelions with small notes of paper, although whether these were requests for favourite tunes of the transvestite doctor's he seriously doubted. Mrs Fox-Vasey's little homily had taken place while Jamie had excused him to visit the gentleman's lavatory. On his return, bowing to the inevitability of the Fox-Vaseys' presence not being a short one, Mortimer had effected introductions. With a brief nod at Jamie, who was clearly not accustomed to being treated like this, particularly by women, excluded from conversations in this way, the awful Ursula then turned her attention to the advantages of sea travel in general and cruises in particular.

All this naturally led her to the obvious question of what Mortimer himself was doing on such a trip. Was he no longer interested in carrying out a 'European operation'? Had he been put off the 'Continental connexion' by his adversary and – as she had subsequently read in the papers – terrorist and gun-runner Pubjoy, whom she had from the very start suspected of being a spy? Or was it Mortimer's own unfortunate imprisonment in Switzerland, perhaps, which had dissuaded him from further missions in Europe? All these questions clearly fascinated Jamie Scott-Munro. Mortimer himself remained mute.

"I understand your reticence, Mr Trippe. It is only natural, but forgive me if I ask you one more thing."

"Please do," Mortimer said, for want of any alternative.

"Since you have now apparently switched your interests, for the moment at least, to the Baltic, might I ask whether you are involved in a similar job here? On this vessel? I shouldn't ask, I know, but curiosity sometimes gets the better of me, I fear."

"No, no, nothing like that. I'm on holiday."

"Well then," said Ursula Fox-Vasey in a blend of disappointment and disbelief, "let us drink to the success of the voyage." Jamie, now glassless for some ten minutes, brightened. Until Ursula clicked her fingers at a waiter and asked loudly for three apple-juices, 'so beneficial at bedtime', and a glass of whisky for her husband who unfortunately was unable to sleep – or claimed to be – without this 'disgusting and unwholesome beverage', although happily his was now the only alcoholic drink of the day.

At half past eleven the apple juice drinker looked at her watch in shock, said it was well past their usual hour but didn't time fly when one was having a thoroughly engrossing conversation? George and Jamie had between them uttered barely a dozen words and Mortimer few more. When the unwelcome intruders eventually took their leave, Jamie turned hollow-eyed to Mortimer. "Chartered accountancy sounds a more interesting profession than I had ever supposed," he said.

"Well you do get the odd overseas trip if you work for a City firm," Mortimer said cautiously. "For auditing and that sort of thing."

"I'd never thought of that," said Jamie. "And now I'm going to have a drink, if I have to pay for it myself."

CHAPTER 11

During lunch with Mr Lamplighter at the latter's club Lionel
had been longing for the meal to finish in order that they
might repair to the Smoking Room, for Mr Lamplighter
invariably declined to discuss business while eating and
Lionel had almost more to disclose to his master than
he could with any degree of composure suppress during
the consumption of what, at the Young Professionals'
Club, passed for food. At last, in the relative comfort and
complete seclusion of the Smoking Room, Mr Lamplighter
ordered coffee and his usual cherry brandy – which Lionel
unsuccessfully tried to decline on the ground of an upset
stomach – and placed the tips of his fingers together in
anticipation. "So, Lionel, you mentioned that you received
two telephone calls during my unavoidable absence this
morning."

"I did indeed, sir. The first was from, Mr Trippe, calling
with his first progress report from the Lucky Lady, the vessel
on which he is –"

"Yes, yes, I know that. But what did he say?"

What Mr Trippe had told him, Lionel said, had been not
only fascinating but probably amounted to a breakthrough
– possibly several breakthroughs, in fact – in the solving of
the most difficult case on which Mr Trippe was engaged …
What it all amounted to, when Mr Lamplighter eventually
succeeded in persuading his clerk to confine himself to the
essential facts – which he never quite did – was something
along the following lines.

In a manner and for reasons never fully explained, Mr Trippe had contrived to exchange staterooms with a gang called the Sink Street Mob. This was obviously a devilishly clever move on Mr Trippe's part since these thugs were as likely as not the hired kidnappers and Mr Lamplighter would immediately see the highly significant implications in terms of possible clues left behind, inside knowledge via the stateroom attendant and so on. Mr Lamplighter saw no such implications, and said as much. Unabashed, Lionel pursued his narrative. Not only had Mr Trippe succeeded in swapping rooms with these ne'er-do-wells, but he had ended up with a room-mate who would all too clearly constitute a most useful connexion in the carrying out of Lady Bertha's assignment. To Mr Lamplighter's continuing mystification, Lionel told how this unusual character who went by the name of Scott-Munro had turned out to be occupying the other of two connecting rooms, which normally formed one large suite. The man Munro had not only recognized the Sink Street Mob at a glance but was clearly familiar with the workings of the underworld in general and that of London in particular and indeed was himself looking for a position on the ship as a bodyguard or similar in order to earn some extra spending money during the cruise, having recently suffered a temporary but quite severe financial setback. It even seemed possible that this man might end up being employed by the kidnap victim himself and since he and Mortimer had already become firm friends, the man would at the very least be useful in helping to identify who the victim might be. A useful contact, to put it at its lowest.

"I see," said Mr Lamplighter, "and has it occurred to anyone that this person Scott-Munro has been planted by the opposition to sow confusion?"

Lionel chose to ignore this absurd remark and ploughed on, informing Mr Lamplighter excitedly but in a manner more confusing than enlightening, of what he understood Mortimer to have told him of some of the other curious happenings during the short time that the Lucky Lady had been at sea:

of the presence aboard the ship of the Sisterhood, of the astonishing appearance of the Fox-Vaseys, of the Estonian quintet and so on, until poor Mr Lamplighter's brain raced and reeled. Lionel's confusing narrative led the proprietor of the Four Eyes Private Enquiry Agency to only one, inexorable, conclusion: of the absolute need for him personally to join the cruise as soon as possible in order to sort out what sounded like a dog's breakfast of the very highest order.

"But you mentioned two telephone calls, Lionel."

"Yes, sir. The second was from Lady Bertha Hook, anxious to know about progress on the case."

Mr Lamplighter did not know whether to feel irritation or relief when he heard that his clerk had declined to tell their client almost anything. On the whole, he felt relieved. He could bring himself to say little more than to give Lionel firm instructions to make the necessary arrangements for him to join the ship at the earliest opportunity.

* * *

As Mr Lamplighter was entertaining Lionel Hawkins to lunch at the Young Professionals' Club in Kensington Square, Lady Bertha Hook was taking luncheon in the more sumptuous surroundings of the Mayfair Ladies' Club off Berkeley Square with the ever-desirable young Cissie Sykes.

Lady Bertha's mood, however, was dark and her brow furrowed. "You will have to speed up the arrangements, Cissie," she said, replacing on her plate a stick of asparagus which she had been on the point of swallowing whole.

"What arrangements, Bertha?"

"Whatever arrangements you have put in hand for our trip to the Baltic. I can't think what other arrangements I have asked you to make."

"Oh that. Well, as I said, there aren't really any arrangements we can make. It's just a question of pitching up at whatever port is convenient and playing it from there."

"I'm not interested in the most convenient port. We must go to the first *possible* port."

"We should just about make it for Oslo, then. Anyway, what's the sudden hurry?"

"I've just had a most disconcerting conversation with someone at the Four Eyes Private Enquiry Agency. *Most* disconcerting. It is clear that no progress whatever has been made on the case. Just book two flights – business class – on the next available plane."

* * *

All that day the Lucky Lady ploughed gamely through the rough waters of the North Sea, not in the modern fashion of her giant sisters (where size alone enabled them to cut through twenty foot waves with hardly a tremor) equipped as they were with stabilizers, anti-roll this, anti-lurch that and anti-whatever else was needed for the perfect comfort of their cosseted passengers, but in the old manner. On the Lucky Lady you knew that you were at sea and there were no illusions about mill-ponds and other aqueous surfaces of undisturbed tranquillity when the truth was that you were in a force 8 gale.

Mortimer was almost alone in walking the decks and using the restaurant for lunch, for most of the passengers remained confined to their staterooms. Their reasons for this were various, ranging from tiredness after the journey to Dover, through over-indulgence in the bar the night before, 24-hour influenza and a host of other reasons of differing degrees of probability, including the mere wish to test out the service in their staterooms. No one complained of sea-sickness.

Jamie sent Mortimer a message via Ramon to the effect that he was, as sometimes happened, for the day a martyr to an unpleasant bout of fibrositis. Since Mortimer knew by now that his new-found friend was a frequent and impervious sailor, he was almost tempted to believe him.

By early evening the storm had abated and the skies were as clear as the seas were calm; all boded well for a normal evening.

"You scratch my back, Mortimer," said Jamie Scott-Munro during dinner, taking another mouthful of the excellent pâté de foie gras, "and I'll scratch yours."

"In what way, exactly?"

"Exchange of ideas and information. Our interests are complementary. I need to establish who on this tub might be willing to pay for my professional services and you need – in the nature of your job I don't obviously know quite *what* you need, except that it must have to do with certain of the less, shall we say conventional of our fellow passengers."

"I see what you mean. So we both help each other?"

"I'll drink to that," said Jamie, holding up an empty glass.

And the Lucky Lady sailed on towards her first port of call.

* * *

On the early morning flight to Oslo Bert (for except in private he would not for some time now be able to resume his preferred persona of Lady Bertha) and Cissie sat back in business class with their first drink. They had been lucky to get seats, Cissie said, and that was only due to a cancellation, mercifully in club class.

"Right," said Bert, "you'd better explain the procedure for going aboard."

"It's more a procedure for nicking someone else's boarding passes, as I told you," said Cissie.

Since Bert had started his career as a 'light fingers' and she herself was not without experience in this field of expertise, Cissie went on, Bert might think that this should not be a problem. But it was by no means as simple as straight wallet or bag-snatching. A number of finer points were involved and were crucial to success. First, the choice of prey: they had to be a pair – of either or each sex – and must share a cabin, for the boarding passes operated also as room keys and keys to different cabins would be useless for a number of reasons; secondly, they themselves must decide what sort of couple they wanted to be and given that Bert had to be Bert and not Bertha in order not to be recognized by the Sisters, Cissie herself would have to be his young partner, either female or male (the latter, she thought, might be more fun); so they would have to go either for a mixed couple or for two men, although there would obviously be a wider choice of the former; also they needed the cabin number and names of the people they would be replacing; and their signatures for signing for drinks and things, as the ship probably accepted no cash.

"But won't it be noticed," objected Bert, "that the buggers have failed to go back on board?"

"Not immediately. I'm pretty sure the passes are the only identification needed. And remember it's still very early in the trip and there will be well over a hundred passengers. I checked that there are no fixed seating arrangements for meals, so it might not be noticed at all except of course by the stateroom bloke. But those characters will swallow any story, however tall, if it's accompanied by a decent enough sweetener." She patted her handbag.

"You seem to have it all pretty well worked out," Bert said, with grudging respect.

"Bear with me, Bert. There's more." And Cissie went on to explain some of the more intricate points.

Bert recognized Cissie's exposition as, in its genre, a *tour de force*, and was confident that nothing could go wrong. Cissie herself was not so sure.

* * *

"Tell you what," said Jamie as he and Mortimer set foot on the quay at Oslo – Jamie, like many of his fellow passengers, armed with an expensive-looking camera – "I'll take you to the Grand for lunch. Far the best place in town."

Mortimer correctly construed this as meaning that he – or, more accurately, Lady Bertha – would take Jamie out for lunch, but he did not demur.

Neither of them noticed, some distance away, a middle-aged man and an attractive young woman apparently idly surveying the dockside scene as the people from the Lucky Lady came ashore.

Coaches had been laid on to ferry the cruise passengers to the centre of the city and Mortimer and Jamie boarded the first one available. From where they were dropped off they walked through some agreeable gardens, with a band and fountains playing, to Karl Johans gate, Oslo's main street, which runs between the parliament building and the Royal Palace. Mortimer was surprised at how peaceful this thoroughfare – and indeed the whole town – was compared with other capital cities he had visited. The Grand Hotel was a solid, early 19th century building both outside and in; for lunch they had a choice between a relatively formal dining-room and an outside café-terrace overlooking the gardens across the street. As much because it was a warm sunny day, with few clouds and a gentle breeze, as out of respect for his client's pocket, Mortimer decided on the terrace, where they found almost the last free seats.

They both ordered simple food and for a change Jamie did not drink more than a couple of beers and half a bottle of wine. They had just ordered coffee when they were approached by a man and a woman, whom neither of them recognized. Both the 50 odd-year-old man and the much younger woman had adopted the simplest, but nonetheless effective of disguises in order to avoid awkward questions later: the man a tweed cap and cheap metal spectacles and the woman a head scarf and wrap-round dark glasses. Both were clearly English.

"Would you mind very much if we sat at your table? There doesn't seem to be anywhere else," asked the young woman, in an accent which she had considerably modified. Despite her camouflage she was by no means unattractive and Jamie was on his feet in an instant, pulling up chairs, shuffling cutlery and ash-trays, even wiping the seat of the chair next to him with a large spotted handkerchief which he drew like a magician from a coat-sleeve, and generally making the newcomers welcome. Mortimer too half rose as the man and woman prepared to sit down. A young waiter swept down on them with an alacrity almost surpassing Jamie's own. It soon transpired that they were on their honeymoon and that their cruise ship had docked at Oslo a little after the Lucky Lady, upon whose quaintness Cissie claimed to have commented more than a little favourably to her husband. (Although neither of them knew it, she and Mortimer, although they had never met, had spoken on the telephone concerning the urgent matter of Lady Bertha's release from Malou Castle, and indeed Bert, in the guise of Lady Bertha, had dinner with Mortimer, but only when the detective was in the guise of Colonel Hetherington. Unlike the lovely black Gloria Ollerenshaw, however, neither Cissie nor Bert appeared to recognize Mortimer's voice and he in turn had not the slightest idea who they were.)

Cissie was sure that Jamie in particular would be easy game, but with every trick that she tried her confidence diminished. Bert himself, although in his younger days an almost unrivalled street pickpocket, did not possess a fraction of Lady Bertha's aplomb and was frozen into virtual inertia by this direct confrontation with his quarry. Cissie went through the whole gamut of the tricks which she had worked out and so carefully explained to Bert on the flight, but nothing produced even the sight of a wallet: her queries about the rate of exchange elicited no more than indifferent shrugs; on the local practice regarding tipping she did no better, for Mortimer simply mumbled that, to save trouble, he always added a little over ten per cent in whatever country or situation he found himself and Jamie, presumably not an enthusiastic tipper, just changed the subject; not even the politest and most solicitous enquiries about the families of the intended victims were rewarded with the merest mention of loved ones, far less any hint of a treasured snapshot. Even when Mortimer paid the bill, he simply handed the waiter a credit card from his jacket pocket and asked the man to add twelve percent for service.

At this point Cissie realized that she was beaten and the two intending fraudsters left to seek more amenable dupes elsewhere.

* * *

Some half a mile from the Grand Hotel, in a less popular part of the city, the Sisterhood was gathered in plenary session, in the basement of an ancient building which had once been a bakehouse but which was now an excellent if little-known restaurant. The basement constituted only a small part of the whole eating accommodation and was windowless and quite Spartan, with one long pine table for eating and two others as repositories for food and drink; there was almost nothing in the way of ornamentation, or even colour. But it had the great merit, so far as the Sisters were concerned, of being quiet and, for the time being private. Elspeth Sturdy had ordered an entirely cold buffet, at which she knew the Norwegians excelled, and local delicacies, mostly in the form of numerous varieties of fish, and unusual salads adorned the tables where food and drink had been generously laid out, to be savoured by the eye almost as much as by the palate. Contrary to Elspeth's strongly expressed wishes, there was no shortage of alcoholic refreshment, and a profusion of tempting looking bottles stood expectantly facing the food. Beside the bottles a small fridge had been specially installed to ensure not only the convenience but the privacy of the English visitors, a polite request having been made that the luncheon party, whose members would be more than happy to serve themselves, should be left in peace. In recognition of his supposed masculinity Cyril Jinks had as usual been deputed to serve the drink, whilst the ladies were happy to deal with their own food, which they did with no little indulgence.

After aperitifs and a small but excellent preliminary course of marinated eel, salted herring and sliced pork in aspic – accompanied, save in the case of Miss Sturdy, by an excellent biting dry white of undisclosed provenance – the teetotaller called for a pause, sensing no doubt from the rate of consumption of the wine, that now would be preferable to later for the discussion of those momentous matters which, to a sane mind, should take precedence over the ingestion of the copious victuals and liquids by which they seemed to be almost surrounded.

"Gloria," barked the leader, draining her glass of grapefruit juice, "I call upon you to make the first contribution to our little gathering."

"Thank you, Elspeth," replied the glorious black lady, "I have something to tell you all, at which I gave no more than the slightest hint when we were in the Piano Bar the other evening."

None of those present, said Gloria, recalling their recent visit to the Scottish isle of Radichsay, could have failed to notice, during lunch on the day of their arrival, an old-fashioned man in his forties sitting on his own in the White Lady Hotel and half obscured by a rather pretty Japanese screen. All agreed that they had indeed noticed this person. They would without doubt, Gloria went on, also remember that this suspicious looking individual had before very long been approached on his sofa by the rather revolting hotel manager, Mr Humphrey Bliss. Again all agreed that this was so and, furthermore, it seemed that all except Cyril Jinks recalled a certain empathy – indeed not to put it indecently (as Dr Mary Wildegoose helpfully suggested) intimacy – developing between host and guest. It was possible, continued the speaker, although by no means certain because of the low tones in which he spoke, that her colleagues might also have noticed the clipped and archaic accent in which the stranger for the most part communicated. Two colleagues had, two had not. The cosy relationship between the two men on the sofa had, however, eventually become acrimonious, as Gloria invited the Sisterhood to recollect, and had culminated not only in a verbal exchange of some vehemence but in actual physical violence. This had indeed by no means passed unremarked by the Sisters, as for sure it could not have failed to do. Gloria paused and looked round the expectant table.

"Now, Sisters," she said, "you may also remember that in the Piano Bar on the ship yesterday evening two men invited Louise and me to join them for a drink. One was obviously a professional charmer that I wouldn't trust further than I could kick, and the other a harmless looking, nondescript sort of chap who let the rogue do most of the talking but did occasionally say something. Now, back to the White Lady Hotel. During the angry exchange between Mr Bliss and the old-fashioned guest, the guest spoke loudly and in a different voice from the one he had used before. This, I strongly suspect, was his normal voice."

"So?" said Elspeth Sturdy acidly, clearly anxious for Gloria's gripping narrative either to finish or to reach some sort of climax.

"So," said Gloria imperturbably, "the raised voice of the guest in the White Lady and the voice of the nondescript bloke in the Piano Bar were the *same* voice. There is no doubt about it. I may not have a particularly good memory for faces, but I never forget a voice. Part of my musical training, I expect."

There was total silence while this sank in. Dr Mary was the first to speak. "Are you telling us that the man half-hidden by the Japanese screen – and no doubt watching us at the luncheon table – and this character in the Piano Bar – who seems invariably to be accompanied by the man whom you no doubt accurately describe as a charming rogue – are one and the same person?"

"That's exactly what I'm telling you. You can draw your own conclusions."

"Thank you, Gloria," said the Chief Sister. "That could be most helpful, though I confess that at present it makes, to me at least, little sense."

"It does to me," averred Dr Mary in a tone which defied contradiction. "Will you permit me to explain, Miss Sturdy?"

"Please do, Dr Mary."

"I smell Lady Bertha behind this," pronounced the wily doctor, to gasps of astonishment and horror round the table. Sisters reached for their drinks and she who now held the small gathering in fearful suspense proceeded. Where had Lady Bertha been while the Sisters were on the island of Radichsay? On the island of Malou. And for what was the island of Malou now renowned, indeed notorious? The attempted theft of the valuable de Lessay collection of paintings. And who had prevented this intended atrocity from being accomplished? An unheard of, indeed almost anonymous private detective from London. And if Lady Bertha was planning some private mischief against her former blood-sisters, to whom would she be most likely to turn? Why, to the best private detective that she could lay her hands on. And from where would she most likely be able to track down this anonymous investigator? On the very island where he had solved this seemingly intractable mystery concerning the paintings, of course.

"Are you all with me?" enquired Dr Mary, her eyes inquisitorially searching the faces round the table, with a particularly hard look at the podgy but apparently just comprehending features of the enormous Cyril. All were, and indicated as much with nervous nods.

"Although I do not know the name of the individual concerned, I know the name of the detective agency by whom he is employed. Even from this distance it should be a relatively easy matter to check whether there is a detective working for that concern who bears the same name as a man on the passenger list of the Lucky Lady. The latter could, of course, be travelling incognito, but that is unlikely. In the time available he could hardly have had time to obtain an alternative passport and the fact that I do not know his name might well suggest that he had no need to. I intend to check and shall do so before the day is finished. Right. Cyril. Coffee!"

* * *

Having paid the bill, and their unexpected visitors to the terrace outside the Grand Hotel having left, Mortimer decided to pay a visit to the gents before he and Jamie also took their leave. His destination was inside the hotel and down some stairs and to get there involved going past the rather splendid hotel dining-room. The entrance being open, Mortimer glanced inside. One look was enough to tempt him in further and, not wanting to look too inquisitive he sat down at an empty table and asked for a menu. The large and well-proportioned 'Norwegian Victorian' room was almost full, mostly, it seemed to Mortimer, with voyagers from the Lucky Lady, presumably the richer ones, for the place was by no means cheap. There were two families, one American with a pretty young daughter of about six, the other English with a handsome blond teenage son; for the rest, they were either couples or groups of three or four, including a number of well-dressed black people. No teeshirts, jeans and trainers here, Mortimer noted with approval. One table, however, surprised him. At it, drinking beer and eating elaborate and presumably not cheap sandwiches, sat a group of half a dozen burly men, all wearing dark and, so far as Mortimer could judge, not particularly well-cut suits; they all spoke English, of one sort or another, and Mortimer was pretty sure that he had seen at least some of them on the ship. They looked quite out of place, but seemed content enough in their own company. After a glance at the menu Mortimer smiled his apologies to the waiter and left. He had had an idea.

Outside, Mortimer sat down just as Jamie was rising to leave. "Hang on a minute," he said. "I'd like you to do something."

"Part of the mutual back-scratching?" Jamie asked enthusiastically.

"I suppose you could put it like that, yes."

Mortimer then asked Jamie to go into the dining-room, in tourist mode armed with his camera, and take some photographs of the room and everyone in it. It had an interesting interior, with murals on two walls and some rather lovely antique furniture so the tourist trick should work for a minute or so at least, he thought to himself. "I want everyone there to be not merely visible on the photographs, but readily recognizable. Every single one of them. OK?"

"Fine. I'll use a flash and a wide-angle lens."

"And here's something for the waiters." Mortimer handed the photographer some notes. "I'll explain what it's about later."

* * *

Back at the quay, Cissie was fuming.

"What the hell's the matter with you?" demanded Bert. "You did very well. We've got what we set out to get. It should all be plain sailing now."

"I said I'd go as your *young* partner, male or female, not as a fucking old frump. Just look at me."

Bert did. "Perfect," he said. "Absolutely perfect."

Although the whole idea of stealing other people's Passcards and assuming their identity in order to go aboard had been Cissie's, Bert had spotted a serious snag. Like most cruise passengers, the average age of those aboard the Lucky

Lady was probably well over fifty and Bert accepted that one more or less nondescript couple in their fifties, armed with the necessary Passcards to get through the security check, would almost certainly go unnoticed. He had no reason to doubt Cissie's assurance that no passports would be needed (although they almost certainly would to go ashore again) and no visual identification required. They had now acquired, after a number of unsuccessful and even embarrassing attempts, all that Cissie had specified as necessary. The rest should be a doddle. Except, it suddenly struck Bert, for one thing: Cissie's looks. She was still in her twenties and, as a girl, her exceptionally glamorous appearance, particularly as a newcomer aboard, would draw every eye; and as a young man, her looks would be no less striking. Although nervous about the whole procedure and so far taking a back seat in the matter which Lady Bertha would have despised, Bert had now put his foot down. It would be mad to jeopardize the whole enterprise for the sake of Cissie's vanity. It had not taken him long to persuade her of the obvious truth of this, but she had been far from happy and now, at the immediate prospect of going aboard, not just for a short time, which could be treated as a rather good joke, but for the best part of two weeks, she was appalled.

The switch from a fashionable young woman in a figure-hugging trouser-suit to Bert's middle-aged wife had not been easy as it was. In the time available Cissie had been unable to find any women's clothes shops capable of equipping her in a suitable manner. It was true that many of the women passengers of all ages wore simple blouses, pullovers and trousers – which were easily purchasable – but these would only have drawn attention to Cissie's young film-star figure and would not for this reason have been appropriate. Finally, at Bert's suggestion and for want of any other option, she had bought a long peasant dress and light shawl and a sort of bonnet – just the sort of things, Bert had assured her, that a tourist did buy in a foreign country, with the added merit that they would lend a degree of anonymity and account for the difference from what his supposed wife would presumably have worn as she went ashore earlier in the day. Her face Cissie had reluctantly attended to with make-up.

But then Cissie had had another terrible thought. What on earth was she to wear for the rest of the trip? She couldn't possibly go down for dinner wearing this garb. Not even once, let alone every evening. Don't worry, Bert had said. For reasons which he had no need to go into, he had brought with him a selection from Lady Bertha's wardrobe. This information had almost caused Cissie to refuse to go aboard at all, but she had allowed herself to be prevailed upon.

Their luggage, if noticed, would have to be explained as souvenirs, bought, perhaps extravagantly, in the market and other tempting outlets in this beautiful city.

CHAPTER 12

Back in their shared suite Jamie proudly produced the photographs which he had taken in the dining-room of the Grand Hotel and showed them to Mortimer. He had had them developed that afternoon.

"Perfect," said Mortimer. "Couldn't be better."

"They are rather good, aren't they? But what on earth d'you want them for?"

"You're looking for some sort of temporary work during this trip, aren't you, Jamie?"

"Yes. I told you so."

"Well, I think you'll find that this photograph includes some if not most of our richest fellow-passengers."

"So?"

"That makes them your potential employers, doesn't it?"

"It could," conceded Jamie, "but have you taken a squint at this lot?" He pointed to the six burly beer drinkers sitting at a separate table.

"Bodyguards, presumably. That reinforces my point."

"But don't you see, you prat," said Jamie with irritation, "that all the jobs are taken?"

"There are nowhere enough of the bruisers to meet the potential demand."

"Meaning?"

"Meaning that whoever hired their own thugs probably did so as a standard precaution and almost certainly brought them with them."

"So the others don't think they need minders, you mean?"

"I think they soon might. Time will tell," said Mortimer. "Meanwhile we've got to find out who's who and which of them employs the plug-uglies."

Mortimer pressed the bell for Ramon, who was there in an instant. Mortimer handed him one copy of the photograph. "Recognize any of these people, Ramon?"

"Some of them, sir. I think they all live in the best staterooms. You want me to find out? I know all stateroom attendants."

A high denomination dollar bill changed hands, "I'd be most grateful, Ramon. I want to know as much about them all as possible. Names, nationality, families, friends on board, anyone they employ –"

"Minders, sir?"

"Yes, Ramon, minders. And if possible what they do for a living and how well known they are – some at least are probably the boastful sort. Also are they big spenders, good tippers and so on."

"I understand, Mr Trippe."

"Thank you, Ramon." Mortimer put his wallet back into his pocket. "The balance on delivery."

"Certainly, Mr Mortimer, sir." Ramon said with considerable enthusiasm. And he withdrew, leaving the worldly-wise Jamie with his mouth agape.

* * *

Until Cyril Jinks's unusually early puberty and his quite unexpected failure to get into his destined Northern grammar school, he had been regarded as a more or less normal boy. The coincidence of these two events, however, had quite suddenly transformed a child of some virtue and intelligence into a lazy, stupid and worthless slob. Having handed in mostly blank sheets of paper at his crucial examination he had not only lost interest in all lessons and games but, in the space of two years, had grown several inches in both height and girth, almost to his present ungainly proportions. Even his formerly doting parents despaired. He himself might, he decided, have lost whatever he had possessed in the way of looks, agility, energy and indeed innocence but he knew that he still owned a sharp and even cunning mind. Feeling no attraction towards girls, and little towards boys either (which in any case would never have been reciprocated) and too lazy to read anything more demanding than comics and gutter newspapers, the young virtual eunuch spent most of his time somewhere between dream and torpor.

One day, however, shortly after leaving school with no qualifications, Cyril had been waddling aimlessly round some of the less salubrious streets of Bradford, his home town, when he had found himself looking into a theatrical costumier's shop window. It had been his eureka moment. He decided that he was cut out for the stage. His parents, who, if not respectable, were middle-class and by no means badly off, had been delighted. Keen as he was to achieve his ambition, the lad had readily acquiesced in being sent to a crammer where, with astonishing ease, he had passed the necessary exams to enable him to enter drama school. So pleased was his father at this quite unexpected development that he started to give his only child a quite generous allowance, which the young Cyril spent mostly on clothes and books about the theatre.

From drama school, however, where the only skill which the budding Olivier had been able to acquire was an ability to speak something passably close to the Queen's English, it had been downhill nearly all the way. In the local repertory company he had come badly unstuck even in the few lowly parts which he had been given and – like many unfortunates before and after him – had decided to see what London had to offer. His short incursion into the theatre had given him one ambition: to live in a mansion, dressed like a lord and surrounded by servants and beautiful objects; for all of which, of course, he would need rather more than his father's admittedly still generous allowance. He moved to the metropolis.

But what was he to do? He was certainly not willing to take a regular and low-paid job, and he had neither the energy nor the skills needed for most types of crime. Any sort of sexual employment was out of the question, as was the entering into any form of human union for gain. Cyril concluded that if he mixed in really low company – which, as it turned out, he rather enjoyed – where enough money, ill or otherwise gotten, was splashing around, some of it might somehow splash on to him. With this ill-formed intention in mind he began to frequent the disreputable haunts of the *demi-monde*, where he felt a certain affinity with homosexuals and transvestites. Realizing that in the London underworld he was unlikely ever to be more than some sort of more or less passive appendage, the by now not quite so young Jinks hid from public view his intellect along with his Northern accent and waited for something to turn up. And one day – or rather night – he met by chance a person who impressed him a great deal. Dr Mary Wildegoose by name, real or adopted. Dr Mary at once recognized Cyril as a potentially useful idiot: first he was, at least nominally, a man, and secondly he was clearly familiar with the identities and workings of London's criminal fraternity. She befriended this odd outsider and started to drop hints about a group of ladies with whom she had formed a partnership and who carried out activities of an unconventional kind, of which the more staid members of society no doubt disapproved, but which were highly lucrative. Might Cyril, she wondered, be interested in being attached to them? A sum of money was mentioned. Something *had* turned up.

Cyril had never doubted that employment with the Sisterhood would, if he kept his ears and eyes open and waited long enough, produce some sort of better opportunity, although he had no idea of what sort. The position with the sisters had proved over the years to be interesting, comfortable, tolerably well paid and to involve little effort. When a man was needed – for Miss Sturdy drew the line at Dr Mary in this capacity. Cyril was there: when knowledge about the criminal underworld was required Cyril, if he did not already possess the information, could find it out; when drinks needed pouring, as they often did, or errands running (well, waddling), Cyril was the man. But now he had had enough, and this sentiment had coincided exactly with his having spotted the opportunity for which he had been waiting; it seemed to Cyril to be an opportunity with almost limitless potential. And it was on the White Lady. He was looking it straight in the eye.

* * *

"Right, Mortimer," said Jamie, as they finished their coffee in the dining-room after another excellent dinner, "how about a quick one in the Piano Bar?"

"OK," said Mortimer. "One. But I've heard from Ramon, and I thought you'd like to know what he's found out."

Mortimer had never known Jamie to finish a drink so quickly as he did his whisky in the Piano Bar; Jamie had suggested a quick one, not a single gulp, but that was effectively what he swallowed.

"We can always have one from the mini-bar," said the thirsty Scot self-consolingly as he stood up.

In their stateroom Mortimer handed his new friend one copy of the lunch-time photographs and took one himself. In preparation for what was to be revealed. Jamie poured them each his customary two miniatures from the convenient little cabinet.

"Right," said Mortimer, "see this slug-like opulent looking bloke at the centre table?"

"Looks promising," said Jamie.

"President of Libya and also, as it happens, part owner of this shipping line."

"Just the ticket, Mortimer. Bang on the nail."

"Except there's a snag."

"I thought there might be."

"A couple of the plug-uglies are his."

"Sugar," said Jamie, who never seemed to use foul language. "I'd forgotten all about the competition."

And Mortimer went through the list, reflecting that there seemed to be little that Ramon and his colleagues in the other most expensive parts of the ship did not know about their well-heeled patrons. One of the black people was a Harvard law professor and, perhaps surprisingly, at least on board, a big spender who, with his pretty young wife, occupied one of the best suites available and who, in spite of his totally different background and nationality and even with his horn-rimmed spectacles, bore an almost fraternal resemblance to another passenger in the photograph. This was apparently the newly elected and soon to be installed Secretary-General of the United Nations who hailed from some small, obscure and far from rich state somewhere in the West of Africa.

"Poor as a church mouse, presumably," said Jamie.

"They think he's on expenses," Mortimer said. "You can probably rule him out."

The father of the pretty young blonde girl was the president of a US oil corporation and that of the teenage boy the wealthy member of an English brewing dynasty: the American had a minder, the Englishman had taken no such precaution.

"A possible runner," said Jamie, and Mortimer continued.

There was a reclusive man on his own with a pronounced German accent who, unlike the others, had not been at all forthcoming about anything: an ostentatious French aristocrat who lived partly in the exclusive *seizième* quarter of Paris and partly in a castle on the Loire who so far had dined alone in his stateroom, largely off champagne, caviar and foie gras, leaving his wife and three children to slum it in the dining-room and who had brought with him a manservant."

"Security, presumably, this manservant," interrupted Jamie.

"Possibly, possibly. Ramon asked, but the chap's stateroom man wasn't sure. You can probably forget him, all the same."

"That leaves two thugs, by my reckoning," said Jamie.

"One belongs to this fellow," Mortimer pointed to an earnest looking man accompanied by a young woman who might, or might not have been his daughter. "A banker who lives on the lake outside Zürich."

"A gnome of Zürich, Mortimer. Would have been just the job. What else?"

"Four other English in a group, two with wives. One of the men is an eminent QC and the other a London banker. And two businessmen on their own. One owns a small supermarket chain and the other a string of chemists' shops, one living in the Lake District, the other in Sussex. Take your pick."

"And that's it?"

"It's enough to be going on with, surely?"

"It's a good start, Mortimer. Thanks. I'll see what I can do."

"And don't forget that they're just the ones who happened to be having lunch in the Grand."

"Best place to go," said Jamie, "as I told you." He paused. "Incidentally, Mortimer, why is it, d'you think, that all these rich buggers have chosen this tub for a cruise?"

"Well," said Mortimer, "none of them look or sound *nouveau riche*, so they'd naturally avoid those flashy modern things with bingo-halls and whatnot. Anyway the food on what you call this tub is first-class and so, if this is anything to go by – he glanced appreciatively round his half of their delightful suite, complete as it was with a large balcony and luxurious furniture and fittings – "is the accommodation. They could do a damn sight worse."

"And so" said Jamie, "could we. Given the spondoolicks, fingers crossed. Don't you think we should have a nightcap?"

Mortimer didn't demur.

* * *

"I want out. And I mean out."

"Don't be so bloody silly, Cis. You can't and you know you can't."

"Just watch me. You think I'm going to stay on this crate, and in this hovel, togged up in a bloody duchess's finery, just to stick my nose out of the fucking cabin. You need your head looking at." She furiously ripped off one of Lady Bertha's finest evening gowns.

Bert glanced round the admittedly inferior 'stateroom' which fate had chosen for them. "You *can't* leave. People don't just pack up a cruise part way through."

"Those poor mutts whose Passcards we nicked did."

"This is no laughing matter, Cis. If you buggered off there'd be a hue and cry when they found out, which they would eventually. They'd want to know why. They'd probably think I'd murdered you. Not without reason," Bert added bitterly.

"I don't care what you say. I'm going."

"And ruin the whole plan? I need you, Cis."

"You could always satisfy your needs elsewhere. Knowing you."

"I need your help, you idiot. Two brains are better than one."

"You always say I haven't got a brain."

This riposte had Bert stumped for a moment. "It's not even two weeks," he eventually said lamely.

Cissie appeared to relent. "I'll stay as far as Copenhagen," she said.

"Short of jumping overboard, you've no option. We're practically there."

"Exactly."

* * *

The Sisters dwelt late in the Piano Bar that evening, deep in discussion, for Dr Mary Wildegoose had just informed the others of her findings. By dint of two telephone calls and the use of an internet café in central Oslo she had established the names of the employees of the Four Eyes Private Enquiry Agency, which included a Mr Mortimer Trippe. On her return to the ship Dr Mary had checked the passenger list. This too included a Mr Mortimer Trippe. *Quod erat demonstrandum.*

CHAPTER 13

Mortimer had now arrived at a most satisfactory accommodation with the breakfast arrangements on the Lucky Lady. The first morning, on his way to where he thought that breakfast could be found, which even at that early hour had taken him along a deck which contained a considerable number of his fellow passengers lying apparently comatose on deckchairs under mountains of rugs and beneath a leaden sky, he had been accosted by a pert but pretty young thing in uniform who spoke with an American accent.

"The healthy breakfast, sir?" she had enquired.

"Oh, yes please," Mortimer had said. "The full whack, you know. Eggs, bacon, sausage, kidneys if possible, the lot. Breakfast like a king, you know, lunch like a lord, dine like a pauper or something like that, isn't it?"

The young lady had clearly assumed that this was the famed British irony which she had heard so much about but never understood and pointed smilingly to some swing doors on the same deck. Mortimer had gone in the direction indicated and, to his horror, found a number of people, some in shorts, some in track suits, others in even more gruesome attire, drinking various unpleasant looking beverages and eating what could most kindly be described as vegetarian food, which Mortimer had chosen not to look at too closely. When he had eventually found the normal dining-room he had been greatly relieved. He had clearly inadvertently taken a route across a deck exclusively used by freaks and cranks – for even the Lucky Lady was not entirely devoid of such people – and he vowed never to come that way again. It had then taken him a little time to accustom himself to the self-service buffet, for he seldom visited hotels where this was the practice, but once he had got the hang of the thing he had been well pleased. There were mountains of eggs, bacon and every sort of comestible that it would be possible to think of to meet the needs of half a dozen or more different nationalities, all served by smiling chaps in chefs' uniforms and all freshly prepared. On the first day he had feasted on the best possible English breakfast fare with scarcely a look at the various cold meats, and cheeses – even pickles –, black bread and other strange confections which foreigners enjoyed for their waking meal. On the second morning, however, he had espied the smoked salmon. Although Mortimer was not actually addicted to smoked salmon – and this was of the highest quality – he was happy to eat as much of it as possible at almost any time of day or night and thereafter it became his invariable breakfast, to the exclusion of all else.

This morning, with the Lucky Lady now docked somewhere in one of Copenhagen's various harbours, Mortimer, when as usual pushing his breakfast tray along the metal rails provided towards the smoked salmon supply, suddenly noticed a mouth-wateringly toothsome young woman in a black trouser suit, whom he was quite sure he had seen somewhere recently but not on the ship. Perhaps she was a shore visitor, for not all Danes had fair hair; possibly even, given what she was wearing, some sort of official. Suddenly, to Mortimer's amazement, this morning vision, who appeared to have been eyeing him up and down, almost as soon as he was seated and had begun to eat his smoked salmon, accosted him in a piercing cut-glass English accent.

"Why, aren't you Mortimer Trippe?"

Mortimer mumbled his assent.

"I was sure of it, from that photograph, though it didn't ring a bell when we met outside the Grand in Oslo. But you weren't eating smoked salmon then and I was sitting opposite you."

"What photograph?"

"The one taken in the Seaview on Malou when you were kissing the barmaid. It may sound odd, but in profile it produced much the same visual effect as eating smoked salmon."

Mortimer remembered that damned photograph now. It was the one in some trash magazine that Emily had taxed him with.

Cissie Sykes disappeared in the direction of the toast-making machine, leaving Mortimer wondering whether he would ever be able to eat smoked salmon again without thinking of that bloody barmaid.

On his return to the stateroom, Mortimer had just flung himself on the bed in order both to recover from his shock and also, if possible, to snooze off the excesses of the breakfast table, when Jamie came in from the balcony to announce that a most frightful commotion of some sort was taking place on the quay. Mortimer joined him on the balcony, and was scarcely able to believe what he saw. Being hustled off the ship by three security men was a long-chinned man wearing a raincoat and trilby hat. He was protesting and expostulating loudly and above the general dockside din Mortimer heard distinctly, in only too familiar a voice, the words 'first class reservation…', 'must protest in the strongest possible terms', '…hear more of this' and 'British Embassy' before the intruder was bundled into the arms of the waiting Danish constabulary. Leaning over the side and cupping his hands round his mouth Mortimer instinctively called out, "Mr Lamplighter!" There appeared to Mortimer to be a brief flutter of recognition in the detainee but after a few moments when the Danish police were obviously debating what to do, Mr Lamplighter was sent on his way with what sounded to Mortimer to be some of the less polite words of the local language ringing in his ears. He was soon lost to sight.

Jamie looked at Mortimer with incredulity. "Do you know that man as well, Mortimer?"

"No. I thought I did for a moment, but I must have been mistaken." It was clear from Jamie's expression, however, that he did not believe a word of this.

* * *

Much to Bert's surprise, Cissie had been as good as her word. Straight after breakfast, she had left the Lucky Lady wearing the trouser suit in which she had arrived in Oslo but also the shawl she had bought there partially to cover her face and enough carefully applied make-up for her brief purpose, before she left the ship. After that she intended to remove both the shawl and the make-up and use her own passport to get past the local customs and immigration people. There was no sign of the bonnet. She had told Bert that she hoped he wouldn't miss her too much, but that it couldn't be helped. She would not, however, be deserting her partner completely. She was not going straight back to London but would, he might or might not be pleased to hear, be the girl in every port, and would no doubt see him each time the Lucky Lady docked. She had enough money for hotels, local flights and other expenses, so there should be no problem. He would have to tell anyone who asked that she was confined to bed and to bribe the stateroom bloke to vouch for this. Bert would understand that she had to take their joint Passcard with her in order to get off the ship, but he could easily replace it. "Toodle-pip, Lady B, see you at the next stop," were her parting words and with a quick peck on Bert's quivering cheek she had been gone. Bert decided to console himself with Lady Bertha's wardrobe and asked not to be disturbed.

* * *

Mortimer had only once before visited Copenhagen, on a short trip with Emily when they had not long been married.

This might prove useful, he hoped, since Emily had always been something of a culture vulture, as was Mr Lamplighter, whom Mortimer was very anxious to find, wherever in this small city he might have gone. There was clearly no time to be lost and Mortimer was ready to leave in minutes. He went on to the balcony and called out to Jamie in the adjoining room, "I'll see you this evening, Jamie. Trip down Memory Lane, so to speak. I spent a few days here with my wife soon after we were married. 'Bye." And before Jamie had time to gather himself, Mortimer was gone.

Being a relatively small ship, the Lucky Lady was moored at an inner harbour and in any case the distances in this sea-girt town were far from vast, so that Mortimer was more than happy to travel only on foot. First, with the help of a map, he made his way to the University Quarter, which he thought might well appeal to Mr Lamplighter as much as it had to Emily, for, apart from the university itself, it contained not only Copenhagen's cathedral, the Domkirke, but the Rundetårn or Round Tower, one of the city's most celebrated landmarks, and a considerable number of museums, all of which left Mortimer personally quite cold. There being, not surprisingly, no sign of the errant investigator at any of these cultural 'musts', Mortimer decided to refresh body and mind with a good Danish beer in the Studiestraede, a narrow 18th-century street awash with antique shops and boutiques whose very commercialism he at least found a pleasant change from the dreary old museums. He felt better for the beer and remembering that Mr Lamplighter had more than once expressed a liking for the town of Amsterdam, he then made his way to Nyhavn, an old and thriving canalside area which Mortimer found reminiscent, at least in appearance, of the now notorious Dutch city.

At Nyhavn Mortimer walked up and down the colourful canal and on the north side he even saw the superb hotel conversion of an 18th-century warehouse where he and Emily had stayed all those years ago. It looked exactly the same as before although Mortimer had quite forgotten its name. From nearby there was a view back over the inner harbour and Mortimer even thought that he caught a glimpse of the Lucky Lady; for some absurd reason he was feeling rather guilty about Jamie. Time for another of those excellent beers, he decided, and settled himself on the waterside terrace of one of the nearby cafés. If Mr Lamplighter was indeed in the area this was probably as good a place to spot him as anywhere else, but Mortimer was not optimistic.

He could only think that his boss must have been trying to board the Lucky Lady, presumably ill-prepared for the strict security, and this could only have been in an attempt to contact Mortimer himself. But why? It was something of a mystery, but if Mortimer had learned anything about the proprietor of the Four Eyes Private Enquiry Agency it was that he did not give up easily. Mortimer guessed that there would be little purpose in now continuing his search and he resolved, therefore to have a decent lunch and make his way back to the ship, scrupulously avoiding both the child-infested Tivoli Gardens and that ludicrous statue of the 'Little Mermaid', which wasn't even a mermaid, so far as Mortimer could judge.

* * *

During the earlier commotion on the quay, Cissie Sykes, who had at the time only just left the Lucky Lady, had heard the shout of 'Mr Lamplighter!' from the ship and she also just about recognized the wearer of the incongruous trilby hat from that disreputable photograph which she had sent for publication (and monetary gain) to *High Society*. Obviously Mr Lamplighter had made an abortive attempt to join Mortimer Trippe on board the vessel and Cissie had every reason for wishing to help him as she was keen for Lady Bertha (as she always thought of Bert), to get her revenge on these bloody Sisters, as they called themselves, and this might well help her to do so. She had therefore decided to follow Mr Lamplighter.

Mr Lamplighter himself, now at large in the town, was in a state of high anxiety. It was imperative that he should board the Lucky Lady, and not merely as a visitor but as a full passenger. Lionel had in fact made him a reservation for this very purpose, but had there been some mistake? It was certainly possible. A repeat of the humiliation which the now semi-fugitive private detective had just endured was unthinkable; the matter needed considerable thought and for this purpose Mr Lamplighter resolved to find a temporary refuge somewhere in the Danish capital. Mortimer's guesses as to his superior's likely preferred locations in that small but beautiful town had been unerringly accurate: the cathedral, university and museum quarter and the canalside region of Nyhavn. With the help of a small guide-book Mr Lamplighter, who was a stranger to Copenhagen, soon arrived at this conclusion himself; but he was in no mood for cathedrals and museums and he decided to seek out instead the more cheerful area of canal-boats and waterfront places of refreshment. Nyhavn was not far and it took the man in the hat and raincoat, a fast walker, little time to gain his destination. It was as much as Cissie, following at a discreet distance, could do to keep up with him, but even in the more crowded streets the bobbing trilby was an infallible guide.

Thus it was that while Mortimer was searching the museums and the University Quarter his fretful quarry was seated at an outside café almost directly opposite that in which the junior detective had himself taken his second beer of the morning. Mr Lamplighter, with his coffee, felt the strongest need for a cherry brandy to calm his nerves and ordered one of these from the American-speaking blond waiter who hesitated only a short time before going inside to obtain this odd Englishman's order. Two minutes later the blond returned bearing on a tray the smallest cup of black coffee which Mr Lamplighter had ever seen and a colossal balloon glass containing the finest – and seemingly most expensive – Armagnac to be had in Copenhagen, into which had been introduced a large measure of very sweet sherry. Mr Lamplighter found this abominable concoction very much to his taste – preferable even to the excellent cherry brandy to be had at the Young Professionals' Club in Kensington Square – and almost with the first sip he felt that it would do something towards healing his wounded spirit. He had, however, obviously only drunk an inadequate amount of the revivifying substance before he was approached by a comely young woman dressed in a black trouser-suit, whom the malefactor guiltily assumed to be from some branch of Danish officialdom. Although the surrounding tables were empty, Mr Lamplighter's worst fears were confirmed when this person brazenly sat down at his own table, smiled ingratiatingly and said: "Good morning, Mr Lamplighter."

Immediately realizing the futility of denial, Mr Lamplighter half rose, doffed his hat and said, "I fear that you have the advantage of me."

"I'm so sorry," replied the apparition. "Cissie Sykes. I don't believe we've met."

"I'm quite sure of it, young lady."

"Do you mind frightfully if I join you? I'm at a bit of a loose end."

"By all means do. Can I get you a drink?" he added as the blond waiter approached with a leer at Cissie.

"I'd love a large gin and tonic, if I may?"

"So be it," said the unintending host and nodded curtly to the blond, who withdrew with more than one backward glance at the unexpected figure in the trouser-suit.

During their brief exchange of civilities while Cissie waited for her drink Mr Lamplighter became convinced that his guest was a genuine English visitor, but he was still puzzled by her direct mode of approach and, not least, by the fact that she knew his name. All, however, soon became more or less clear. Not only had Cissie heard his name called out during the commotion on the quay but she recognized him from a photograph taken in a bar on the island of Malou a few weeks ago which she had seen in a London magazine. She knew from the accompanying article that he was the head of the detective agency which had solved the de Lessay art mystery and that Mr Mortimer Trippe, who was now a passenger on the Lucky Lady, had also been involved in that matter. It looked to her, she said, as though Mr Lamplighter had been attempting to board the cruise ship, presumably to join his subordinate, but that something seemed to have gone wrong with the arrangements.

"You are quite right, Miss Sykes," said Mr Lamplighter. "My clerk had made a firm booking for me to join the ship here in Copenhagen but quite inexplicably, as you may have observed, I was turned away and indeed not only roughly manhandled but forcibly ejected from the vessel like a common criminal." In his distress at recalling this intolerable event Mr Lamplighter took a considerable slug from the fearsome potion which stood at his elbow, and Cissie gratefully swallowed more of her large gin and tonic, which by English standards, although unknown to her, was a quadruple. Her next words almost took her host's breath away.

"It so happens, Mr Lamplighter," she said, "that due to the strangest circumstances, I may be able to help you to join the Lucky Lady's Baltic cruise."

"God bless my soul," ejaculated the proprietor of the Four Eyes Private Enquiry Agency in astonishment. "Perhaps you would care to explain?"

And Cissie did, not entirely untruthfully. She had, she told Mr Lamplighter, in secretive tones and looking about her furtively, come to Copenhagen to meet her lover, a Dane of true Viking stock and even now a seafaring man of whom her parents disapproved for a number of different reasons which it was not necessary to go into. Her father had always wanted to see the Baltic ports and had suggested that she

126

should accompany him on a cruise to these beautiful waters at a time when she had happened to mention that her Dane would be away at sea. Her father was a disorganized man who had left the booking rather late, with the consequence that they had been obliged to fly to Oslo and join the ship there. But there had been a problem. Although they had reason to believe that there was always the odd empty stateroom in case of emergencies, and that a kind word with the relevant steward would secure one of these, assisted of course by a modest gratuity to the purser, they had not realized that it was impossible to board the ship at all without a thing called a Passcard which doubled for use as a room-key. This was where Cissie had to confess that she had misbehaved in a most shameful way. Anxious that her father, who was recovering from a recent operation, should not be disappointed, and she herself desperate to see her Danish lover, she had had no option other than to take from a middle-aged couple, whom she and her father had met in an Oslo café, their Passcard and other effects while the husband had gone 'to see a man about a dog' and his wife 'to powder her nose', during which time these unfortunate people had left the lady's handbag on the table for Cissie and her father to keep an eye on. They would, of course, be fully insured, but even so Cissie felt that this might rather have spoilt their holiday; she felt profoundly guilty about the matter, for it was the first time that she had ever done anything remotely like this, and would certainly be the last. In fact the thing had been done pretty much on the spur of the moment; what she had sometimes heard described as an irresistible impulse. Cissie had taken only what was necessary from the handbag, leaving the bag itself and its monetary contents where its good owner had left it; she had, however, been careful to take the couple's address in Dorking and fully intended to make amends so far as was humanly possible, even at the risk of being reported to the Surrey police. But that, continued Cissie shame-facedly, was not the totality of her wrongdoing.

Her father had insisted that his daughter should not even attempt to go aboard the Lucky Lady looking her normal self, for she would be far too conspicuous among the other passengers, who were mostly middle-aged or elderly. She had, therefore, equipped herself with a shawl and a Norwegian peasant dress – the sort of thing that a female tourist bought every day in Oslo – in order to look, so to speak, like her own mother. But all along, to her shame, but for the sake of an overwhelming passion, she had intended to disembark at Copenhagen, the next port, and leave her father to his own devices. She fully understood that not only would the poor man be lonely and worried, but he would now be at risk of exposure as an impostor and worse once it was discovered that his 'wife' had vanished into thin air. But on arrival at the quay, her Viking lover had not, as he had promised on his mother's grave that he would be, been there to meet her, and here she was, pouring her heart out to a virtual stranger: desolate, lonely and full of the most appalling remorse. Theoretically, of course, she could now rejoin the ship but in practice that was not possible. Despite the evidence, she was convinced that the Viking was somewhere in Copenhagen and she was resolved to find him, whatever the outcome. All that she could now do to help her poor father was to find for him a replacement, whose presence would avert the ignominy of detection in what had undoubtedly been a deception and perhaps afford him some comfort in his distress. Did Mr Lamplighter understand?

Cissie swallowed more of her gin and tonic and Mr Lamplighter took an enormous gulp of his sherry brandy. His mind was in a veritable tumult. He had a glimmering of understanding, but also the gravest reservations about embarking on such a questionable enterprise. On the other hand, if he had understood correctly, this was the only conceivable chance that he had of gaining passenger-status access to the Lucky Lady, which after all was the sole purpose of his having come to Copenhagen and indeed, from what

Lionel had told him, also the only way of saving Trippe's assignment from abject failure. Furthermore, a reservation had been made for him – and paid for – so that it was clear enough to Mr Lamplighter that, whatever the technicalities of the situation, he was morally in the clear. But from what this admittedly charming young lady had told him, it seemed that there was one insuperable practical difficulty. During a long and so far unblemished career as a private investigator Mr Lamplighter had of necessity been obliged on not a few occasions to adopt disguises of one sort or another. Indeed he fancied himself as something of an expert in the practice. But never as a woman! And, initially at least, as a Scandinavian peasant woman. To board the vessel in this guise might just about be tolerable, but what of the rest of the cruise? Must he for nearly two weeks appear to be Cissie Sykes' mother and a total stranger's wife? But, he supposed doubtfully, there was always the chance that he might be able to find accommodation of his own, once things were sorted out.

He vouchsafed his fears regarding his new identity, including what he would have to wear, to his guest.

"Oh, don't worry about that," Cissie said with a breezy wave of her free hand. "Once you're aboard you can obviously wear what you like. It's only for embarking and disembarking that you have to be careful. It'll be a doddle."

In his anxiety to join the Lucky Lady it may be that the eminent detective accepted these assurances too readily. However that may be, the shawl, the peasant dress and the Passcard and other documents changed hands and Mr Lamplighter set his jaw in determination. On Cissie's advice, he decided not to join his ship until early evening, when most of the passengers would be returning and he would merely be one of a crowd. He felt more optimistic and ordered further drinks. He had always enjoyed the company of pretty young women.

* * *

In a little-known restaurant not far from the Amalienborg Palace, suggested to the Sisters by their supposedly confidential secretary in London, who had carried out extensive research into all the ports which they were to visit, the Sisters were once more taking what Elspeth chose to describe as a 'business lunch'. This time, far from being in a basement, they were at the very top of the building with extensive views across Christiansholm and the inner harbour in which the Lucky Lady had docked and they could clearly see her waiting for their safe return. Again they had a private room but this time Elspeth Sturdy – although a virtual teetotaller by no means a vegetarian – had eschewed the cold table offered and advised something more sustaining, a suggestion which the Sisters were happy to go along with.

As usual, Elspeth opened the proceedings: although the leader of the pack, she had the good sense to know which of her team best served what purpose; she herself was far and away the best on matters of detail and organization; Gloria could be relied upon to judge the vagaries of human nature, good and particularly bad; Louise was their expert on all matters French, although her skills had never been called upon since the Sisters had so far not even considered operating in France or indeed in anything which might have involved French culture or the French language; Cyril was an invaluable contact in anything concerning the very lowest layers of society, and his knowledge in this area was indeed by no means infrequently invoked; when it came to matters of extreme complexity and deviousness, however, where sheer brainpower was needed to unravel them, Dr Mary Wildegoose stood alone. And it was to the learned doctor that Miss Sturdy now turned.

"While you are consuming your apéritifs," she said, perhaps a little pointedly, "I shall ask Dr Mary to summarize for us the present position, as she sees it."

"Thank you, Miss Sturdy," and Dr Mary looked severely round the table to ensure that no mind should wander. "The situation, as I believe I intimated to you all earlier, has become more involved than we could have wished. We decided while on the island of Radichsay not only that the Chameleons should be our blunt instrument, but also that, in order to avoid any breach of security, they should not be informed of the when, where, and, most vitally, the whom until as late as possible and that this information should be communicated to them by Cyril, who knows them and was of course instrumental in our obtaining their employment. Of Lady Bertha's evident intention and of her engagement of Mr Mortimer Trippe to implement it we have already touched upon.

"Two other matters, though, again thanks to Cyril," and here Dr Mary politely inclined her head to the invaluable male member of the group, "have been brought to my attention. First, the highly undesirable looking gang of four obvious criminals whom you cannot have failed to observe on the ship are, it seems, known – no doubt with good reason – as the Sink Street Mob and are not unversed in the practice of kidnap. For this reason it could be inferred that Lady Bertha has also engaged them, with or without the knowledge of the sleuth Trippe, to assist her in her vile objective. One way of achieving this would, one may assume, be to seize or incapacitate our target before the Chameleons go into action, although there could of course be other methods, and you may rest assured that I am giving the most careful thought to all alternative possibilities. The other complicating factor is that the man Scott-Munro, who seems now to be the almost inseparable companion of Mortimer Trippe, is not unknown to London's criminal fraternity and conversely Scott-Munro himself apparently makes it his business to know a good deal about the toughs and ruffians of South and East London and he will undoubtedly know of the so-called Sink Street Mob, if not also of the less notorious Chameleons." Here Cyril nodded wisely. "The whole thing," concluded Dr Mary, "presents something of a tangled web upon which at present I do not propose further to conjecture."

"Goodness gracious me," said Elspeth Sturdy. "I would only –"

But she was interrupted by Gloria Ollerenshaw. "Any road," said the delectable black Sister, "let's refill our glasses," she paused while Cyril obediently performed this function, "and drink to our success. *Skål*!"

Cyril Jinks smiled inwardly . He had just had yet another rather good idea.

* * *

"Good morning. Or is it afternoon?"

Cissie looked up. It was her Danish lover! Just as she had imagined him. She was almost speechless.

"Oh, hello," she said, trying to sound casual.

"If you prefer being on your own … I have no wish to intrude."

"No, really. I'm not waiting for anybody." For want of a better place, she had gone back to the outside café where she met Mr Lamplighter.

"In that case?" He pulled up a chair.

"Please do."

And he did. He had conventional Scandinavian good looks, with blond hair, blue eyes and regular features. But not the almost dummy-like appearance of some men – and women for that matter – with supposed good looks.

"Can I get you another one?" he asked

Cissie thought. "I'd better not have any more gin. This is only my second but I'm already beginning to feel a bit squiffy. I'd love a beer, though."

The man half turned his head and called out over his shoulder, "Two beers, please." He still spoke in English and Cissie was not sure whether the waiter had heard. "I'd better introduce myself," he said. "Per Carlsson."

"Hello again. I'm Cissie Sykes."

"You're English?"

"Yes. And you? Swedish, to judge by your Christian name."

"Yes. Very much the Viking."

Curiouser and curiouser! "You from Stockholm?"

"Everyone asks that. I'm from the Åland Islands originally but I live on my boat."

"So you just sail around the Baltic?"

"Mostly the Baltic. Occasionally further. Usually on my own but sometimes I take fare-paying passengers to help with the budget. Then I have a couple of crew."

A seafaring man to boot. It was almost unbelievable. The beer came, so the waiter had heard.

"This is all most extraordinary," Cissie couldn't help herself saying, "because I invented you less than a couple of hours ago."

"Invented me?"

"Well, I hope you don't mind, but I made you up as an excuse to discourage an older man who seemed to be trying to pick me up. On this terrace, as it happens."

"I'm curious. Who was I?"

Cissie paused, affecting embarrassment. "My Danish lover, actually."

The Swede laughed. "Well I'm neither Danish, nor your lover, so it can't have been me."

"Not quite," said Cissie, perhaps a little tendentiously.

And they talked, and had another drink, and talked some more and finally Per glanced at his watch. "My God," he said, "time for a bite of lunch."

And he took Cissie to a cheap bistro, which he insisted was 'his treat' and then on a sight-seeing tour of Copenhagen, which he knew well – well enough to avoid the Tivoli Gardens, he said, and, like Mortimer, to give the horrible 'Little Mermaid' a wide berth.

She'd really fallen on her feet, thought Cissie. Per the genuine article, not a professional charmer, thank God – although he was by no means lacking in the quality – pleasant, bright, knowledgeable, by no means tight-fisted and with excellent colloquial English. He might not be a Dane but as to the other main ingredient of her imagined Viking, she would see.

* * *

Mortimer returned to the quayside about an hour and a half before the Lucky Lady was due to sail. And so, judging by the throng jostling each other towards the gangplank, did most of his fellow passengers. Only a few paces in front of him, Mortimer's attention was attracted to the sight of a woman wearing a shawl and a long peasant dress. He was sure that he had seen this person before but now something struck him as odd. Whoever was draped in this strange costume looked taller than previously and the shoulders broader – too broad possibly even for a hardy Scandinavian peasant woman, which this individual in any case obviously was not. The woman appeared to peer about her rather furtively, almost guiltily, and seemed to be in an undue hurry to get aboard. But when Mortimer looked down, he observed the most bizarre feature of all – beneath the too short dress protruded a pair of men's brown brogue shoes.

Could this be a putative stowaway or illegal migrant of some sort – even a potential terrorist? Whoever it was must somehow have stolen the clothes of the genuine female passenger to whom they belonged. Mortimer decided to follow the man – for a man it unquestionably was – who, furthermore, was carrying a suitcase which might contain the heavens only knew what. At the machine into which it was necessary to insert one's pass, the suspicious looking creature was clearly unsure what to do and, instead of inserting the card, handed it to the security girl. She put the card in herself and duly removed it and handed it back to its non-owner when it reappeared. And then, quite unsuspectingly, she waved the impostor through. Once on board the female impersonator was even less at ease. Mortimer himself found the signs indicating the deck levels and stateroom numbers a little confusing, but it was soon clear – as Mortimer expected – that this was the criminal's first time on board the Lucky Lady. Mortimer pulled his straw hat close over his eyes and continued his pursuit, of which the man in the shawl remained clearly oblivious. When eventually he found the correct stateroom he had even more trouble opening the door with the Passcard than even Mortimer had had at *his* first attempt. At the moment when he succeeded, and threw the door open with relief, his pursuer, the Panama now obscuring half his face, was immediately behind. What private investigator Trippe now heard and beheld caused in him emotions too profound for expression by even the most elegant of poets.

Preening herself before a full-length mirror, and indeed wearing the same dress which she had worn when Mortimer – as Colonel Hetherington – had dined with her in the Castle Hotel on Malou, was Lady Bertha Hook. At this sudden incursion her ladyship almost shouted, in a male voice with an East London accent: "Jesus Fucking Christ Almighty!"

At the same time, a voice which Mortimer could not fail to recognize, exclaimed, "God bless my soul," and its owner quickly shut the door.

* * *

After the town sightseeing tour Cissie and her 'Danish lover' were rather thirsty and decided to have a beer. They were in Kongens Nytorv – the 'King's New Square' of Christian V and the city's largest square, Per explained – and he pointed to the wonderful façade of the Hotel D'Angleterre.

"It's supposed to be one of the finest hotels in Denmark," the Swede said, "but to my shame I've never even set foot in the place. In view of your nationality I think we should give it a try, don't you?"

"Fine," said Cissie.

When they had finished their beer, Per said, "I'd much rather spend the night here than on my boat. It would make a lovely change. How about you, Cissie?"

After suitable prevarications and the usual hypocritical discussion about one room or two, Cissie said that she would love to, agreeing in particular that one room would be cheaper than two, but also insisting that it was a condition that they went 'Dutch'. Per would hear nothing of this: it was simply a question of Viking hospitality, he said; he was the host and she was the guest.

And so it was. Per booked a room and left Cissie to get ready while he went back to his boat to fetch some more suitable clothes. And then dry martinis in the bar were followed by an excellent early dinner, with champagne. The host ordered coffee and Armagnac in the room and asked the waiter to leave the bottle to save him the trouble of coming back, at the same time slipping him what looked to Cissie like a pretty generous tip.

It was all too good to be true.

CHAPTER 14

After breakfast the next morning Jamie came into Mortimer's room and sat down uninvited. Mortimer, replete as usual at this time of day with smoked salmon, was not anxious for conversation. Jamie, on the other hand, seemed to be bursting for human association.

"Well that was a fine thing, Mortimer, buggering off and leaving a chap completely on his tod at only the second stop. I was totally spare all day."

"You mean you had no cash to go anywhere?" Mortimer asked with uncharacteristic if perhaps justified cynicism.

"That's not what I meant at all." Jamie sounded piqued. "I've just got used to your company, that's all. What happened to you? What were you up to?"

"I explained all about that before I left," Mortimer replied, once more feeling absurdly guilty.

There was an uneasy silence, eventually broken by Jamie. "You're holding back on me, Mortimer. There's a lot you're not telling me."

"There's a lot you're not telling *me*," replied Mortimer evenly. In fact you're one of the most secretive blighters I've ever come across."

The Scot ignored this and lit an illicit cigarette. "Who, for example, was that dishy young woman you were chatting up at breakfast yesterday?"

"I wasn't chatting her up. She spoke to me. Just two passengers passing the time of day."

Jamie almost choked on cigarette smoke. "That's a porky for a start. She knew your name. I happened to be within earshot and I heard. In fact half the people on this ship seem to know you."

Mortimer recognized that, although this was something of an exaggeration, it was not without foundation. Gloria Ollerenshaw knew him – or at least his voice – and so did the wretched Ursula Fox-Vasey and both had made this all too clear in Jamie's presence. And now young Cissie Sykes. And then of course, there had been the quayside commotion involving Mr Lamplighter. None of which was to say that Jamie did not also know some of those aboard, or know of them: the Sink Street Mob, for example and no doubt various of the other less reputable passengers.

Mortimer was annoyed to have been caught out in what was with little doubt a lie, but what could he say about Cissie?

"She recognized me from a photograph," Mortimer said.

"Very likely," replied Jamie. "A holiday snap?"

"All right, all right, I once spoke to her on the telephone."

Jamie laughed out loud. "And you say you didn't know her?"

"I never actually said that," answered the accused.

"You certainly implied it. And you told me she was just another passenger, which she certainly wasn't, or I would have recognized her. I hadn't seen her before and I haven't seen her since. I wish I had."

Mortimer knew that he was cornered. "Well she's a friend of someone I'm doing a job for, but I'd never met her before."

"And now she's disappeared?"

"She seems to have done, yes."

"And she's a pal of the Director-General of MI5?"

"Don't be so damn silly."

"It's not me that's being silly, Mortimer. Examine your conscience."

This really riled Mortimer, as no doubt it was intended to. Worse, he knew that there would be further probing questions and that yet again he would get caught out. He had never been any good at dissimulation. Where would be the harm in telling Jamie at least some of the truth? He couldn't tell him about Lady Bertha's assignment, of course, that was confidential, but the fact of being a private investigator, now he came to think about it, wasn't exactly classified information. He'd want something of a *quid pro quo* from Jamie, naturally. After all, they had agreed to help each other and they couldn't very well do that without something to go on.

"OK, Jamie," he said, "I'll explain. Provided that you also tell me about *yourself.*"

"Fair enough," said Jamie, "though there's not much to tell from my side, I'm afraid."

This sounded highly improbable to Mortimer, but he decided to go ahead notwithstanding. He disliked unnecessary secrecy and anyway it might be useful to have someone to talk to. He was particularly puzzled about what he had witnessed in stateroom number nine when he had followed the hooded Mr Lamplighter back from the quay late yesterday afternoon. That didn't seem to have any particular bearing on Lady Bertha's assignment or anything else that was confidential, for that matter. And so he told Jamie Scott-Munro about his twenty year servitude as a chartered account, his by no means unwelcome dismissal from the wretched firm of Hicks & Briggs, his subsequent short and ill-fated coach tour with Eurolux Tours and his fortuitous employment by Mr Lamplighter of the Four Eyes Private Enquiry Agency.

"So that's where the mysterious Mr Lamplighter fits in? He was trying to join you presumably, before he was chucked off the boat?"

Mortimer found himself on the defensive again. "I don't know. I haven't communicated with him."

Jamie looked at Mortimer with the utmost scepticism, as he stubbed out his cigarette in a fruit bowl. "But you must have tried to contact him?"

"I looked for him, but with no success."

"So you haven't seen him since the episode on the quay?"

"Well –"

"Well?"

"Well, as a matter of fact I did see someone who turned out to be him when I got back to the quay. But in disguise."

"In disguise!" Jamie was ecstatic. "Don't leave me in suspense, Mortimer. I can't bear it."

"Yes, well it was a bit odd actually. He was wearing some sort of female peasant kit and I followed him onto the ship. When he got to his stateroom I was directly behind him. After some initial difficulty he opened the door and there was a very grand looking duchessy sort of a woman preening herself in front of a mirror. At the sight of Mr Lamplighter, she swore terribly but in a man's voice and with an East London accent."

"Perfect," said Jamie. "Absolutely perfect. Do go on."

"I was certainly surprised, Jamie, I can tell you that. Anyway, there's nothing more to tell. Now it's your turn." But even as he spoke Mortimer realized that telling Jamie of the extraordinary scene in stateroom number nine had suggested to him a possible – indeed probable – explanation for what he had witnessed, and even for his earlier encounter with Cissie Sykes. If that wasn't proof that honesty was the best policy, Mortimer was blessed if he knew what was.

* * *

When Mr Lamplighter had closed the door of stateroom number nine behind him the previous evening, he had expected – or at any rate hoped – that the creature confronting him, with the appearance of a high-born lady but the voice of a ruffian, would somehow become transfigured, if only into one or the other. This was not, however, to be so. Instead, tearing off the top half of its fine apparel and thereby exposing an unquestionably masculine torso, it at once became a fabulous being for, heightening its strange appearance, it now spoke in the distinctly female tones of the English nobility: "I must be going quite mad," it said, and Mr Lamplighter shuddered and shook in the profoundest shock.

Lady Bertha for her part was scarcely less composed. Had she been expecting anybody – which she certainly had not – it would have been the absconding Cissie and at first her ladyship took the hooded figure to be her. The size of the unlooked for intruder cast the first doubts as to its identity but the extraordinary voice transformed these into incredulity. Who or what was this person and how had it acquired a Passcard to the cabin and come to be wearing the same disguise which Cissie herself had used to board the ship in Oslo? It was because of the extreme consternation which Bert felt at the sudden entry of the grisly apparition that he had unthinkingly started to tear off his female attire and for the same reason that Lady Bertha had begun to speak in her own voice.

And then for a full minute neither of the participants in the nightmarish spectacle uttered. Mr Lamplighter was the first to break the silence. In an almost normal voice, his upbringing coming to his much-needed aid, he said: "I believe that we should introduce ourselves. I am Hereward Lamplighter, proprietor of the Four Eyes Private Enquiry Agency of Kensington, London. Forgive me if I intrude."

Lady Bertha – Bert could not have done this to save his life – responded in kind. "Lady Bertha Hook of the Mayfair Ladies Club when in London, and of Hook Manor, Devonshire, when in the country. How do you do?"

These announcements astonished each as much as the other, for both were familiar with the names spoken but unable to associate them with those who had spoken them. Again there was silence.

"Eventually, with some effort, Mr Lamplighter said, "my firm has a client by the name of Lady Bertha Hook, but –"

"And I have instructed a firm which goes under the name of the Four Eyes or some such … But –"

Again there was an impasse, which it took more than a few moments to resolve. Acceptance of their respective identities by the two adversaries was never quite achieved but, not without considerable misgivings on both sides, there was some sort of grudging acquiescence. This did not, however, at first extend to the roles which they were each to play for however long it might be that they should have to endure their joint incarceration in this by no means extensive 'stateroom'. Both forcibly expressed their reasons for needing to play the part of what they claimed to be their own sex and on this, much to the chagrin of Mr Lamplighter, Lady Bertha had the final word: if she were not the man, she argued, both their interests would be irretrievably wrecked for she would at once be recognized by the very people whose dastardly plans they were both aboard the Lucky Lady to abort.

* * *

In the luxurious bed at the Hotel d'Angleterre, Cissie woke late. She put out an arm for her Swedish lover but found his side of the bed empty. He must be in the bathroom she decided, and nodded off again. But when she next woke up it was nearly ten o'clock and there was still no sign of Per Carlsson. She snatched up the bedside telephone and dialled reception. She was told that her husband had checked out two hours ago as he had an early meeting, which he'd forgotten to tell her about. He apologized, but hadn't wanted to wake her up. He would meet her at noon in the waterfront bar where they'd had a drink yesterday. He was afraid that due to pressure of business he wouldn't be able to spare long for lunch, so would Mrs Carlsson please settle the account with reception before she left, to save her husband time?

Cissie could have howled. She'd been completely taken in. How could she have been so bloody stupid? And the bill at this place was going to be astronomical! But she would have to pay it, there was no getting out of that. What a bastard!

CHAPTER 15

On board Mortimer and Jamie usually took lunch separately.
Today was fine and much warmer than most people seemed
to expect in the Baltic for September, so Mortimer decided to
eat beside the swimming-pool. He had always been confused
by the various decks on boats, even on cross-Channel ferries,
and he was never sure whether this was the same deck where
he had seen all those idiots swathed in rugs on his way to
a 'healthy' breakfast the first morning, which he had sworn
never to go near again. Anyway there was a small bar there
near the pool, run by a pretty young Caribbean girl called
Blossom, where he sometimes stopped for a beer or a glass
of wine. There was also a hamburger bar and since Mortimer
had never had a hamburger in his life (Emily would have
been appalled at the idea) he decided to try one now.

"Hello, Blossom," he said. "Beer weather, I think."

"Sure. Why not?"

"Then I thought I'd try a hamburger. I've never had one
before."

This simple remark provoked in Blossom an explosion of
total disbelief. When at last she was convinced that she was
not having her leg pulled, she insisted on superintending the
preparation of Mortimer's meal, for she had taken something
of a fancy to this rather odd Englishman who, even by the
standards of the Lucky Lady, was always dressed a little more
formally than was usual. Today, Mortimer wore a Panama hat,
long-sleeved shirt and white cotton drill trousers, whereas
most of his neighbours had settled for short-sleeved shirts,

shorts and sandals or tennis shoes (tee-shirts were frowned upon and 'trainers' strictly forbidden). Mortimer asked for his beef rare and not to be wrapped in one of those disagreeable looking buns and for the customary chips and salad, and it all proved excellent. He really must try to convert Emily, he decided. But his mind was really on other matters.

He was thinking about the sudden realization that had hit him after breakfast when he had been trying to account to Jamie for various odd occurrences: for the fact that yet another passenger, this time Cissie Sykes, obviously knew him and that she had now vanished as mysteriously as she had appeared; for Mr Lamplighter's equally strange appearance on the quayside and Mortimer's own subsequent fruitless search for him; for the figure in female peasant garb who later boarded the ship; and finally for the extraordinary spectacle which he had witnessed in stateroom number nine. Mortimer's realization as to what all this meant had been so sudden, and in hindsight so blindingly obvious, that he could not imagine how he had not thought of it before. All these events pointed in one direction only. He had known all along, of course, that young Cissie Sykes was a *protégée* of Lady Bertha Hook and Cissie had told him in the breakfast queue that Lady Bertha was herself on board. And as the strangely dressed Mr Lamplighter had entered stateroom number nine Mortimer had with his own eyes seen Lady Bertha vainly examining herself in the mirror, albeit that she turned out to have a man's voice, and a very crude one at that. It seemed to follow that her ladyship, for whatever reason, was merely adopting some rudimentary subterfuge in order to try to disguise her true identity, as indeed was Mr Lamplighter. Furthermore, when Mortimer had seen the hooded proprietor of the Four Eyes Private Enquiry Agency guiltily shuffling aboard the Lucky Lady he had remembered having seen a similar, but smaller, figure boarding the ship at Oslo. On reflection this could only have been Cissie Sykes who must then have lent her odd disguise to Mr Lamplighter so that he himself could now go aboard, having failed at his first attempt. Cissie must also have given Mr Lamplighter her Passcard both to get through security and to open the door of stateroom number nine, where, for whatever reason, she had caused him to change places with herself and share a cabin with Lady Bertha Hook. It all made some sort of rather odd sense. He decided to leave for later the puzzles as to why Lady Bertha Hook and Mr Lamplighter had come aboard in the first place.

So much for that enigma. So far, at least. But it did not even begin to start to deal with the kidnapping business, which after all was why he himself was aboard the Lucky Lady. It seemed to Mortimer that there were two main matters to resolve concerning this. First, who were the actual kidnappers, for it was obvious that the Sisters themselves would have engaged someone else to do their dirty work? And second, perhaps more importantly, whom did they intend to kidnap? How to prevent this happening could not even be considered until he had an answer to the first two questions.

As to the likely kidnappers, assuming that they would be some sort of gang or group as opposed to a loose cannon or loner (in this connexion, Jamie had briefly crossed his mind as a possibility, but he had quickly dismissed the notion for a number of reasons) there seemed to be only two sets of contestants; the Chameleons or the Sink Street Mob. The Chameleons looked as though their origins lay elsewhere than in England and Mortimer had heard them early one evening in the Champagne Bar talking between themselves in a language which Mortimer didn't recognized. When he had asked them, the Beak had told him that they had been speaking Estonian for practice and that although they were now Londoners they had all been born in Estonia from where they had fled with their parents while that country was still under Communist rule. This work as ship's musicians was a good chance to see their place of birth for the first time since their escape as children, and to be paid at the same time;

hence their practising the language. Further, the invaluable Jamie had told Mortimer that he knew that the group hovered somewhere on the fringes of the London underworld. (So, it seemed more than possible, did Jamie. When it came to his turn to give a fairly brief history of his own background he had merely told Mortimer that he had been at school at Gordonstoun with Prince Charles, but only just, as 'Charlie Boy' was, of course, several years older – and after school had been commissioned into the Scots Guards from where he had transferred to the SAS and served as a troop commander in the South Atlantic before going on to serve in other places which it was not necessary to mention. On resigning his commission he had had various jobs but for the most part had been at something of a 'loose end'.) The Chameleons therefore, presumably with local connexions in Talinn and the ability to speak the language, looked like the front-runners, if, that was – which on the whole seemed likely – the kidnap was to take place in Estonia; Mortimer also knew that the Estonian and Finnish languages were similar to the point of being mutually intelligible, so he did not rule out Finland as the possible venue of the 'snatch' either; furthermore Mortimer knew from looking at an atlas in the ship's library that off the west coast of Finland, not far from Helsinki, there were literally myriads of islands – far more even than those which he had already seen off the coastal waters of the Baltic itself – many of which were small and presumably uninhabited, and one of these would seem to be no bad place to hold a kidnap victim during 'negotiations'. Apart from these various reasons Mortimer had seen both the huge Cyril, of the Sisterhood, and Dr Mary hand up written notes to the Chameleons in the Piano Bar late in the evening. Cyril's role in the Sisterhood was far from clear to an outsider but the women seemed to treat him as some sort of subordinate and the role of messenger and dogsbody was quite consistent with this; neither Cyril nor Dr Wildegoose seemed the sort to make musical requests of their own and anyway, if the notes were such, why the secrecy? It struck Mortimer that the Sink Street Mob – obvious criminals to their fingertips, for a start – would be very much a second choice. Mortimer's money was firmly on the Chameleons as the kidnappers.

Identifying the target looked like being a much tougher nut to crack. Mortimer had memorized the people on that photograph in the Grand in Oslo, and what Ramon had said about them, pretty clearly and had had no need to bring it with him. A preliminary point, of course, was whether the target necessarily appeared on the photograph at all, for surely it would be asking a lot to assume that all the richest and most important passengers on the Lucky Lady had happened to stumble on the Grand Hotel for lunch on their one day in Oslo? But he had discreetly checked this point with the seemingly omniscient Ramon, who had supplied an explanation which seemed to Mortimer to be as plausible as could be hoped for, if not *quite* conclusive. Anxious for rich custom, the Grand Hotel always asked the stateroom attendants serving all the suites on board to leave its brochure in a prominent place and also to make personal recommendations. Mortimer knew, if only from his brief experience with Eurolux Tours, that, for a consideration it went without saying, this sort of thing was a common practice; it also accounted for Jamie's unexpected suggestion that the two of them should have lunch at the Grand, for when they had arrived in Oslo it had soon become obvious that Jamie had never been there before in his life. Ramon had also confirmed that – as was by no means invariably the case – all those who had taken suites on this trip had been to the Grand for lunch, as was evidenced by that rather good photograph. With one exception: a very old Russian lady who never left her suite. Ordering another beer from the obliging Blossom, Mortimer brought the photograph into sharp focus in his mind's eye.

Since all those with bodyguards had clearly brought them with them when they boarded the ship at Dover it followed that they had been booked on the cruise well in advance of departure. The Sisters would have been able to establish this without too much trouble for they clearly had underworld connexions and would hardly have chosen a target who was already prepared in advance, particularly since the Chameleons, although no doubt highly suitable in their way for the job on hand, did not seem to Mortimer – or from the admittedly small amount that he had established from Jamie – to be the sort who would be able to deal easily with professional thugs. Mortimer, working on this assumption, decided to rule out: the slug-like President of Libya and owner of the Lucky Lady's shipping line; the president of the US oil corporation with the pretty young daughter; the French aristocrat with the 'manservant'; the Zürich gnome; since no one seemed to be sure whether bully-boy number six belonged to the supermarket man or to the chain of chemists shops man, Mortimer could not afford to exclude either. Apart from these two, there were left: the Harvard professor with the pretty wife; the Secretary-General-elect of the UN; the English brewer with the teenage son; the recluse with the German accent; the eminent QC; and the London banker. That was eight men, some with wives and one with a son. Quite a range of choices, thought Mortimer, and decided to look at them one by one.

Mortimer knew quite well that what the whole thing boiled down to was not so much the wealth of any particular individual or family as how much money could be extorted in exchange for their safe return. The fact that they were all in expensive suites could obviously reflect their importance just as much as their personal wealth, for appearances counted with such people; in some cases their expenses would be paid for by employers or associates, which could also point to their relative worth as kidnap victims. The two black men scored well according to these criteria. Harvard was a rich university and would pay highly for the return of a law professor, for its law faculty was one of the most prized in America; also, with their obsession with racial politics, the

Americans would probably pay more for a black professor than for a white professor and no one could charge them with racial discrimination for that!

Mortimer had, only in the last few minutes as it happened, developed a strong feeling about the United Nations man, although he could not at the moment quite put his finger on it. During his long wait for his first assignment with the Four Eyes, Mortimer had become something of a 'newsfreak'. Not only had he had time on his hands but he had assumed, quite correctly, that a close knowledge of current affairs should stand him in good stead in his new work as a private investigator, and had bought and avidly read as many newspapers and journals as he could lay his hands on. This had continued as something of a habit ever since and he remembered reading something about the election of the new Secretary-General of the United Nations quite recently, although he could not exactly remember what it was. He knew that it would come to him sooner or later and put the thought to one side in order to continue down his list.

Next was the English brewer with the teenage son, aged about thirteen or fourteen, Mortimer guessed, and, if anyone in this family, a possible target. At dinner Mortimer and Jamie quite often sat near enough to the Sisters to overhear some of their conversation – never obviously 'shop' – and it was clear that Dr Mary, who was the brains of the group would probably have selected the victim; but Dr Mary clearly not just detested children of all ages but had such a profound dislike for them that she wished nothing to do with them. Not that this in itself would have ruled out the young lad as a kidnap target, although the doctor would presumably have been aware that many boys of this age were inclined to relish any situation involving their idea of adventure and to be hot-headed even in some cases to the extent of being almost impervious to danger, which could obviously be problematic for any kidnappers. What in Mortimer's opinion did exclude the boy, however, was Gloria Ollerenshaw's ridiculous sentimentality towards children of any age under about seventeen and it was clear that the black Yorkshire woman's views carried considerable weight within the Sisterhood. The lad could safely be dismissed as a possibility. Next, no one would pay a huge sum to rescue a recluse, so the man with the German accent went out too. After him came the QC and the banker; but their money would be their own and probably not accessible to others for use for hostage release; their wives could be taken, of course, but the QC's wealth such as it was, apart from probably tied up pension pot, would be more likely to be income than capital, and there was no reason to suppose that anyone else would have the necessary money, or even the wish, to pay for his freedom. The banker also would not necessarily be all that capital rich and his obviously wealthy employers would have no particular reason to fork out millions on his behalf, bankers these days being ten-a-penny. Mortimer wondered whether he wasn't being rather cynical, but one had to be hard-headed in these matters. Forget both the QC and the banker, then. Mortimer couldn't definitely exclude the supermarket man or the chemist shops man, but he had a hunch that neither would be much of a catch, which brought him back to the Harvard law professor and the United Nations man; what *was* it that he had read quite recently about the latter's election as the new Secretary-General?

"Another beer, sir?" Inevitably it was the ever-attentive Blossom, but Mortimer inwardly cursed the girl for having interrupted his train of thought.

Another beer, however, might help. "Yes please, Blossom. One more would be just right," he said, and even as he spoke it came to him. The recent election to replace the retiring Secretary-General had been a close-run thing. Mr Ntoko, as the new man was called, Mortimer had read, was no friend of the Russians or the Chinese and apparently quite incompatible, and the Russians had at one stage threatened to veto his election but had backed down eventually after some quite unpleasant exchanges. Moscow's preferred choice, who was also looked on favourably by the Chinese, had been voted second and, if for any reason Mr Ntoko were unable to take up his position in just over a month's time, would inevitably replace him as the new Secretary-General. God, thought Mortimer suddenly, almost unlimited amounts would be paid for Ntoko's release, particularly by the Americans and the other NTO members of the Security Council. The shrewd Dr Wildegoose presumably knew all this and the other Sisters would have blessed her for her choice and thanked their lucky stars that Mr Ntoko had chosen to go on a cruise leaving from the United Kingdom before taking up his post. So far as Mortimer was concerned the question of the target was concluded and with a grateful smile at Blossom as she brought his beer he settled back to enjoy it.

CHAPTER 16

It was not long before Mortimer realized the next day that his smoked salmon breakfast was not destined to be the peaceful affair that it should have been.

First Jamie, who Mortimer knew to be an early riser and whom he had never previously seen at the morning meal, joined him at his table with a brief apology for doing so but explaining that he was famished after his 'work-out' in the gym and in need now of spiritual nourishment, as he had not spoken to a living soul all the previous day, until dinner that was, and coming straight after having been abandoned to his own devices in Copenhagen, it was a bit much. Did Mortimer suppose that he had come on holiday to spend day after day talking to himself? Now that they were docked in the German port of Warnemünde he had decided to catch Mortimer before he crept off again in that secretive way that he had and he himself was once more left on the Lucky Lady like a beached whale. He had seen some 'bumf' in the stateroom about a little restaurant in nearby Rostock which was cheap and cheerful and also, on Saturday afternoons, had jazz; he would, for a change, be more than happy to treat Mortimer to lunch there although, with the euro being the euro, they would probably have to settle for a glass of beer and share a bottle of plonk. Before Mortimer had even had time to thank Jamie for this quite unexpected invitation, another intrusion occurred. A middle-aged man of somewhat uncouth appearance came up to the table and, without any preliminary courtesies, said, "You are Mortimer Trippe, aren't you?"

Jamie looked frankly astonished and Mortimer did not dare to guess what might be going through his mind. "Do I know you?" he faltered.

Certainly you know me. Only quite recently I – well it was me, even if you can't see it, if you see what I mean – entertained you to dinner at the Castle Hotel on the island of Malou. In somewhat different circumstances, admittedly."

Mortimer thought quickly. The only person whose guest he had ever been at his former place of employment on Malou was Lady Bertha Hook. But then he had seen Lady Bertha on this ship only two days ago when Mr Lamplighter, whom mysteriously he had not seen since, had gone into her room disguised as a peasant woman. So … So? So what did it mean? But in her stateroom Lady Bertha had for some reason been affecting a man's voice. This man? And then it came to him. It must be this man and of course, Mortimer remembered, when he himself had been Lady Bertha's dinner guest he himself had been in the guise of his own grandfather, Colonel Hetherington. Fair was fair. But how did this rude blighter now recognize him? Partly because he did not wish the matter to appear to Jamie more bizarre – sinister, as the Scot would no doubt see it – than necessary, he decided to give away as little as possible. "I have been to Malou, certainly," he said.

"Of course you have and for –" The man stopped himself. "In case you are wondering, Mr Lamplighter described you to me. It was a very accurate description. He wishes to see you in our shared – er, accommodation, as soon as possible. Number nine." And with this Bert turned abruptly and walked away.

"But wasn't that the bloke who joined us outside the Grand in Oslo, with the dishy bird who was supposed to be his wife? He was wearing a cap and specs at the time but I'm pretty sure it was the same bloke, disguised or not," asked Jamie, as Bert left.

"God," said Mortimer. "Was it? That chap was sitting next to me and I never got a full view of his face. Are you sure?"

"Sure as eggs is eggs. I expect you were too busy eyeing up the girl. At the time I thought they were after our wallets. They certainly asked some very odd questions."

"Good Lord," said Mortimer. "Anyway, I'd better be off." And he swallowed a final mouthful of smoked salmon as he stood up.

"You haven't forgotten our lunch date?"

Mortimer had, but he said, "I'll see you back in the room in half an hour."

"Bit of a rude bugger, your pal, wasn't he?"

"I think he's rather mixed up," said Mortimer. "One way or another."

In stateroom number nine Mortimer found Mr Lamplighter in thoroughly evil spirits. "At last, Trippe," said the proprietor of the Four Eyes Private Enquiry Agency, "you condescend to visit me."

"How was I supposed to know that you were aboard?" asked Mortimer disingenuously. He found matters confusing enough without Mr Lamplighter's quite unnecessary intervention and he would have been happy to let him kick his heels for the first couple of days, although he was puzzled as to why there had been no sign of him.

"Were you not informed of my presence?"

"Only five minutes ago," Mortimer said, with perfect truth.

But Mr Lamplighter was not so easily to be mollified. "I am imprisoned, Trippe. Incarcerated by some gruesome transvestite, who I now understand to be our client. That, at all events, is this person's claim. It is insufferable. Indeed it is outrageous. For someone in my position it is wholly without precedent."

"But you don't need to stay in your stateroom, surely?"

"Stateroom! You dare to call this a stateroom? It is more like a prison cell, Trippe, which I am forcibly obliged to share with a creature of the most devious sexual proclivities."

Mortimer was horrified. "Surely Lady Bertha doesn't er –"

So appalling was the thought which had crossed his mind that he was unable to express it.

"He – she – the sexual identity of my captor appears to change almost by the minute." Mr Lamplighter flung open a wardrobe, packed to bursting point with the finest ladies' clothes. "Look at these, Trippe. Just look at them."

"I can see them," said Mortimer. "They are Lady Bertha's clothes."

"Which, whenever the urge moves him, this pervert parades in up and down the cell."

"Yes, well, if he went out in them the Sisters would recognize him as Lady Bertha and the game would be up. And our assignment with it."

"*Your* assignment, Trippe. Your assignment. It was your rashness which brought this humiliation upon me."

"But why do you have to stay closeted in here? Why don't you go out? It's not as though you're physically restrained."

"Not physically, perhaps, but restrained nonetheless. By blackmail. Our so-called client – *your* client – refuses to let me go out unless I dress as a woman. Which I utterly decline to do. Apart from which I have no female apparel save a peasant outfit of ludicrous aspect, so I would have to be seen in those." Again the distraught detective pointed to Lady Bertha's ample, if ornate, wardrobe.

"But why?"

"Because I have to appear to be my captor's wife. Otherwise he claims that he would be exposed as an impostor and – at best – thrown off the ship at the next port."

"Would that be so terrible?" asked Mortimer, who would have been more than happy to see the back of Lady Bertha.

"It would, Trippe. It would. For in that eventuality, your client threatens that our fees would be withheld. A not inconsiderable sum and, of course, all expenses incurred."

Mortimer understood. As usual, the firm's fees were never far from the forefront of Mr Lamplighter's mind. "I see," Mortimer said. "It is an unfortunate situation."

Mr Lamplighter smiled bitterly and peered out of the small, salt-encrusted porthole, for there was no sweeping balcony here. "I intend to go ashore at this port, however unpromising it might look. I shall wear a shawl and that absurd dress for the boat's security people and remove them before passport control."

"Quite," said Mortimer. "Well, I'll see you later, Mr Lamplighter."

His superior merely snorted.

* * *

Cissie was waiting for Bert when he got off the ship and, as soon as he was through customs, rushed up to him and flung her arms round him.

"What on earth's the matter with you?" demanded Bert, now suspicious of everything and everyone.

"Nothing," said Cissie, bursting into floods of tears. "Nothing at all," she sobbed.

Bert looked round frantically. "And for Christ's sake stop blubbing. Everyone's looking." Indeed they were and Bert, still fearful of detection for whatever reason, thought reasonably enough that this scene did not greatly contribute to the appearance of normality which he was at pains to create; it was bad enough having two wives without one of them, albeit perhaps now looking a little different, bawling her bloody head off in public.

"It's just seeing you," wailed Cissie ambiguously.

The most that Bert was able to extract from the distraught young woman was that she had had her credit card stolen, for she obviously could not tell him the truth, but was now penniless.

"I'm sorry I left you, Bert. I really am. Anyway, don't worry, I'm coming back onto the ship with you, whether I have to dress up in Lady Bertha's clothes or stay in the cabin, I don't care. I'm coming back."

"You can't, you stupid cow. Mr Lamplighter's sharing with me now, and there's no way that hole is big enough for three of us."

"But I've got to. I'm completely destitute," howled Cissie.

"Let's get away from this dump at least," said Bert. "We'd better go into Rostock and think about it."

* * *

It took Mortimer and Jamie little time to conclude that, despite the extravagant praise of its virtues contained in the brochure from the Lucky Lady, there appeared to be nothing in the port of Warnemünde beyond the docks, a shopping mall and a small railway station. Seeing no sign of Mr Lamplighter, Mortimer suggested that they should go straight to the station and catch the first train to Rostock.

Almost the first person that they saw on the platform was Mr Lamplighter, who presented a most curious appearance. On his head he as usual wore his trilby and, except for a wary expression, looked almost normal from the neck up, but he was dressed in a long sort of woman's peasant dress, which Mortimer supposed at first he must for reasons of his own have purchased in one of the many souvenir shops in the shopping mall, until he remembered that it looked very much like the outfit which the poor man had been wearing when Mortimer had followed him to stateroom number nine, when he had also set his astonished eyes on the apparently hermaphroditic Lady Bertha. Mortimer drew attention to the dress, which caused Mr Lamplighter to appear even more ill-at-ease.

"God bless my soul!" exclaimed Mr Lamplighter, looking down. "I had to wear it off the ship, of course, and there was nowhere to disrobe, so to speak, before customs, but I think that they must have taken it to be an example of English humour. They did not smile, true, but at least I wasn't arrested.

I'd quite forgotten that I was still wearing it. I'd better take it off. Where should I go, Trippe?"

Mortimer pointed to a sign saying 'HERREN' and Mr Lamplighter, with a doubtful glance at the 'DAMEN' went into the gents. When he emerged he was looking much like his usual self and seemed to think that he and Mortimer had arranged to meet on the railway platform. It was only a brief train ride to Rostock, but a longish walk from the station when they got there. Ever since meeting Mr Lamplighter, Jamie had looked apprehensive and Mortimer guessed that this was because he suspected that he would now be entertaining two guests, not one, to his cheap and cheerful lunch. Rostock proved to be a mediaeval delight, fully up to the promises of the brochure. Despite severe bombing during the Second World War and a 45-year Soviet occupation after the end of it the mostly Gothic and Baroque buildings in the centre looked to be in perfect condition; even the replacements of those destroyed during the war were hardly distinguishable from the originals. As soon as they reached the centre Mortimer suggested a beer, on him, partly in order to mollify Jamie, whose despondency lifted immediately at the mere proposal. Rather to Mortimer's surprise Mr Lamplighter and Jamie appeared to take to each other quite readily and the local brew could not be faulted, least of all on the ground of size. It took them little time to find Jamie's chosen restaurant which surprisingly for somewhere so cheap was in the huge, partly cobbled market square almost opposite the perfect façade of the *Rathaus* or Town Hall. It was certainly a cheerful place with long refectory-style tables, presumably designed to ensure maximum conviviality. Jamie and his guests were barely seated before they heard a youthful female cry from outside and Cissie, who had obviously seen them through the window, rushed in, reluctantly followed by Bert, and sat down directly opposite Mr Lamplighter.

"Mr Lamplighter! Mr Lamplighter! You remember me?" blurted out the young woman in anguished tones.

159

"Of course I do, my dear," said Mr Lamplighter consolingly.

"I badly need your help, Mr Lamplighter. Only you can save me."

Bert looked distinctly embarrassed and the others puzzled.

"How can I do that, young lady?"

"Well, for me, just for me" – and here Cissie assumed her most helpless and pleading damsel-in-distress expression, with a flutter of her eyelids for good measure – "I wondered, Mr Lamplighter, whether you might be an angel."

"What d'you want me to do?" enquired the detective, now more than a little rattled.

"What I need more than anything in the world," urged Cissie, "is to rejoin the Lucky Lady."

At this possible glimmer of hope, Mr Lamplighter looked more interested and raised his eyebrows. Cissie then explained that she was really Bert's wife, not as she had claimed when she and Mr Lamplighter had met in Copenhagen, his daughter, and that the story she had told him then had not been strictly accurate but that in her extreme distress at the time she had told him the first thing that had come into her head. In reality she and Bert had had something of a domestic tiff and the only thing that could now restore their marriage was for her to go back to him immediately. There was no possible way that she could do this without Mr Lamplighter giving up his share of stateroom number nine – like the chivalrous gentleman that he undoubtedly was – and thus allowing her to resume her rightful marital position, even if she may have behaved a little less than perfectly, for which she now apologized publicly and unreservedly to all concerned, particularly to her beloved and much wronged husband.

"Well, I – er, the way you put it, my dear, I shall be only too happy to oblige." Mr Lamplighter, in his anxiety to be out of that blasted cell once and for all, with no loss of face or fees, chose to overlook any improbabilities in Cissie's account of the matter. "Yes," continued the senior detective, "I shall be happy to make this sacrifice for such a charming young lady." Cissie climbed onto the table and gave her benefactor a huge hug.

Bert, considerably relieved to be rid of the constantly complaining Mr Lamplighter and glad, although he would not of course admit it to her, to be getting Cissie back in return, having first apologized to Mortimer for his abruptness at breakfast, said that in gratitude he would make a gesture; the meal and drinks, including during the afternoon jazz session, would be on him. This handsome suggestion naturally delighted Jamie and so, with Mortimer also thankful that Mr Lamplighter would be getting out of his hair, all were satisfied. The meal went well, even if Jamie's suspicious about Mortimer were once more raised by the fact that he unthinkingly conversed in fluent German to a group of locals at the same table.

When they were about to leave, Mr Lamplighter told Mortimer that he now proposed to catch a train to Berlin, a mere 150 miles away, which he had always wished to visit. There, for the sake of completeness in the matter of the de Lessay collection riddle, he would visit the crumbling mansion which he understood still belonged to Graf Heinrich von Schwarzenhof Zu Stolp, whose guilt in that affair, along with that of his fellow conspirators, Mortimer Trippe had eventually managed to prove.

* * *

Mr Lamplighter's progress towards the door was suddenly checked by a loud shout.

"Mr Lamplighter! Mr Lamplighter! I'd quite forgotten. I shall need those clothes I lent you in Copenhagen to get back on board."

"Unless, which I much doubt, they have been purloined, you will find them, young lady, in a rubbish bin on the south-bound platform at Warnemünde railway station. The

161

bin is situated midway between the gentlemen's and ladies' lavatories. I bid you all good afternoon."

* * *

That evening back on board Mortimer and Jamie dined together, as usual. They had now also developed an almost invariable routine after dinner. First, they would have a couple of whiskies in the Piano Bar – as often as not with an extra one for Jamie – and then they would go for a stroll on the upper deck, provided, in Jamie's case, that the weather was fine, preferably with a moon and a starlit sky. Mortimer would go on his own in even the worst weather, otherwise he had difficulty sleeping; Jamie solved any possible problem of his own in this respect from the mini-bar. Mortimer, a man of habit, invariably wore for these nocturnal deck walks his Panama hat and carried his black, silver-tipped cane, both inherited from his paternal grandfather (not Colonel Hetherington, who would not have been seen dead thus equipped) from whom he had also copied the on-board ship night walk habit with hat and cane. If it was wet Mortimer wore instead of the Panama a black straw hat, which he claimed to be waterproof and which, he thought, went rather well with the cane.

"Usual?" said Jamie after they had finished their meal. "Piano bar and deck walk?"

"I'm pretty whacked after that day in Rostock," Mortimer said. "I'll join you for a quick one in the Piano Bar but I think I'll skip the walk tonight, if you don't mind."

"Fair enough," said Jamie, for although it was a fine evening he was never averse to staying a little longer in the bar.

When Mortimer, after the promised drink, rose to leave the bar it was already quite depleted. Some of the Sisters were still there and Cyril Jinks was as usual talking to the barman, presumably once again weary of female chit-chat. When Jamie, instead of beckoning the waiter, went up to the bar to get another drink, Cyril greeted him. They knew each other by sight and reputation from the shady London clubland that both frequented.

"Can I get you one?" asked the big man and received the not unexpected enthusiastic affirmative. They talked desultorily for a while, but when the last of the Sisters left the bar, Cyril suggested sitting down, and this they did.

"Skint as usual, Jamie?" Cyril asked pleasantly.

"A bit, yes. Always on the lookout for something."

"There's something you might be able to do for me," said Cyril. "You probably think I'm one of that gang of women, but I'm not really. More of a dogsbody, almost a bloody manservant in fact. Always running errands and stuff for the bitches. I'm not badly paid but I need more of the readies, like you, and this time they've asked me to do something which might earn me some Brownie points from them and maybe some dosh on the side."

"So?"

"It's only a possibility, see?"

Jamie pricked up his ears. "Try me," he said.

"Are you a great mate of this Mortimer Trippe bloke, I was wondering?"

Jamie's sixth sense came swiftly into play. "I wouldn't say a great mate exactly. Shipboard acquaintances. Drinking pals, if you like. We're both on our own and happen to be in the same stateroom."

"Yeah, I know."

"So?"

"Well, the thing is, might you be prepared to do something a bit, shall we say, to Trippe's disadvantage, if there was enough dosh in it?"

"It would depend," Jamie said carefully. "What is it?"

"It's only a bit dodgy. No real harm."

Jamie swallowed the rest of his whisky as Cyril summoned the barman, the waiter now having gone off duty. "Fire away," said Jamie.

"Well, you know the Sink Street boys?"

"I know of them, yes. Nasty bastards."

"Yeah. Right …"

CHAPTER 17

The next port of call, Tallinn on the coast of Estonia and that country's capital city, was, so far as Mortimer could work out, something like 400 miles from Warnemünde and, since the Lucky Lady's cruising speed was around 14 knots, this meant that they would now have two consecutive days at sea. Mortimer was grateful for the prospect of a little peace after the various dramas of the previous day; it would give him time to take stock. The last time that he had given the complexities of his assignment any serious solitary thought had been over his first hamburger lunch prepared by the delightful Blossom. That occasion had produced some ideas and he decided to try the same recipe again.

Blossom was delighted to see him and indeed had set in motion the necessary preparations for his lunch almost before Mortimer had so much as ordered a beer. The weather was cloudy and the swimming-pool mercifully quiet; Jamie claimed to have a headache (a hangover?) and had remained in bed so that Mortimer was pretty much alone with his thoughts. As soon as he put his mind to the job in hand the first thought that crossed his mind was how little he had achieved. He had tentatively concluded two things: first, that the kidnappers would be the Chameleons; and secondly that their target was probably the Secretary-General elect of the United Nations. But these conclusions, even assuming that they were valid, left a large number of gaps and unanswered questions. As Mortimer drank his beer and watched from a safe distance as his hamburger fizzled and spat under Blossom's watchful

165

eye, the questions occurred to him in no particular order; and as they did so his attempt to resolve the whole matter seemed increasingly hopeless.

What, for a start, were the Sink Street Mob doing on board? If they were up to no good, then who had hired them and for what purpose? Why had Lady Bertha joined the cruise, obviously at short notice? Had she come in an attempt to abort the Sisterhood's kidnap attempt and if so how, and why had she not told him? Had she herself hired the Sink Street cutthroats in order to pre-empt the Chameleons in their kidnap bid, and how could she do this without knowing who the target was? If she *did* know, how had she found out and why had she not told the very man she had engaged to scupper the Sisters' scheme, namely Mortimer himself? Was it because for some reason she did not trust him, and if she didn't why was this so? Lady Bertha was obviously disguised as Bert – or was it the other way round? – for the benefit of the Sisters, but this did not explain her presence on board in the first place. What, if any, was Jamie's role in all this? Was he to be trusted? (Sometimes Mortimer was convinced that he was, at others equally convinced of the opposite.) He clearly hadn't found work as a bodyguard and, as far as Mortimer could see, he hadn't even tried. So had his Scottish friend some other scheme in mind or was he just lazy? And then there was Cyril. Not only was he set apart from the others by not being a woman, but Mortimer had the impression that the Sisters treated him more as a minion than as a partner; and, importantly, he was, according to Jamie, the gang's main contact with the underworld. He would probably know, or know of, these Sink Street characters, and possibly of the Chameleons as well. He even seemed to know Jamie himself, at least by sight. So what, if anything, did all this mean? The more Mortimer thought about the pieces in the jigsaw the more of a puzzle did the whole thing seem. Ah, but there was his glass of red wine, quickly followed by the hamburger. He hadn't even needed to order the wine.

"Thank you, Blossom. It looks delicious."

"It ought to be. Let me know when you want another glass of wine, Mr Trippe."

With relief, Mortimer allowed his mind to stray from the various problems while he ate and drank. The sun was breaking through the cloud and it was now quite clear, so that he could easily make out the coast to what he forced himself to think of as starboard. Poland, he reckoned, from his map. But now the blasted sunbathers had come on deck and Mortimer decided to force his thoughts back to his assignment, before his mind went a complete blank, which it had a habit of doing in surroundings which he found uncongenial.

He had not, of course, so far even considered the main difficulty. Even supposing that his existing suppositions were correct, and that none of the possible problems and queries which had occurred to him was insuperable, how was the attempted kidnap to be stopped or in some way aborted? Strong-arm tactics were out of the question unless, that was, he enlisted Jamie's assistance, but that supposed several things: that the man could be trusted; that he would be prepared to help and on reasonable terms; and that he would be capable of doing what was necessary. Had he really been in the SAS, or even the army for that matter? Even if he had, he would still, not counting Mortimer himself, be outnumbered by four or five to one. No, force looked to be out, even if he could establish the precise time and location of the attempt at the snatch. That left subterfuge. But what sort of subterfuge? It was easy to think of the concept in general terms, but a carefully worked out plan – and a good one – would be needed and at present Mortimer had not a single idea in his head as to how such a tactic might be put into effect. He asked Blossom if she would be good enough to bring him another glass of wine. He had concluded almost nothing and they were inexorably approaching Tallinn, one of the two most likely places for the attempt – if it was only an attempt.

Before dinner Mortimer went into Jamie's room to see how he was. He was still lying on the bed looking extremely sorry for himself.

"Not coming down for dinner, Jamie?"

Jamie sighed. "Ramon's bringing me something in here," he said. "He suggested a plain omelette and a glass of mineral water."

"Well, let's hope it does the trick. I'll come up straight after dinner to see how you are."

Jamie grunted his thanks and Mortimer left, realizing that he did not much relish the prospect of dinner on his own. Lunch on your own was fine, he thought, or even dinner in a quiet restaurant with a decent book, but not in this place. He needn't have worried, however, for he had hardly sat down before he was approached by Bert, looking quite respectable for a change in his dinner jacket, and offering a friendly greeting.

"Mind if I joint you, Mr Trippe?"

"Delighted," replied Mortimer. "It so happens that Mr Scott-Munro, my usual dinner companion, is indisposed."

"Not sea-sick in this weather, surely?"

"No, no. A minor stomach upset, I suspect. He'll be OK by tomorrow. Anyway, do sit down."

Bert insisted on buying a bottle of excellent wine which, Mortimer reflected, albeit in the shape of Lady Bertha, he would have paid for anyway and, after some general chat about the cruise, including the fact that Cissie was in a difficult mood and had also ordered something in their stateroom, Bert got down to business. He naturally did not wish in any way to impede Mortimer's investigations, he said, or to distract him from his important objective, but he wondered whether the detective could give him an idea as to what conclusions he had so far reached. Lady Bertha was anxious to know, he said disconcertingly, as though the forthright noblewoman were somehow a different person, which of course, in a way she very much was. Mortimer thought hard before answering. It was not a question that in any event he would have welcomed from a client in mid-investigation, but since in this case he had at this stage come up with only two positive thoughts, which left open far more questions than they answered, he was especially reluctant to discuss his progress. On the other hand it would appear churlish to give no answer at all, and could even look as though he had even this far into the cruise drawn a complete blank. After a careful look round to ensure that he was not overheard, therefore, he told Bert of the two points on which he was now reasonably sure, namely the identities of both the kidnappers and the victim, including the deductive processes by which he had arrived at these answers. Bert seemed both pleased and impressed, particularly by the shrewdness of taking a photograph in the Grand Hotel in Oslo of the most likely candidates and of the reasoning behind Mortimer's belief that the UN man was to be the chosen hostage.

"And the where and when?" enquired Bert.

"It's a little premature for that," Mortimer said stiffly, aware as he said it that it was not in the least premature, as they were fast approaching what Bert, given the nationality of the Chameleons, also had every reason to suppose was the most likely venue for the event. At almost the same instant the detective was struck by a much darker thought. If Lady Bertha really had hired the Sink Street Mob to make a pre-emptive strike, Mortimer had just told her alter ego whom to seize. He quickly changed the subject.

As good as his word, Mortimer gave the Piano Bar a miss and after dinner went straight back to the stateroom. What he found was, to say the least, surprising.

Now fully dressed and sitting in his favourite chair beside Mortimer's mini-bar, Jamie Scott-Munro looked to be in the pink of health, and was drinking a glass of whisky and water.

"Well, you certainly seem to have recovered, Jamie," Mortimer said.

"Ramon's a magician. I never thought an omelette and mineral water was likely to do a man much good, but in this case it did. I think he must have put something in the water, even though it tasted just as foul as mineral water normally does. Care for a scotch?"

"Certainly," said Mortimer as Jamie, without needing to move, produced a bottle from the mini-bar.

"My God! What on earth was that? You'd better have dekko outside, Mortimer."

Mortimer had heard nothing. But he dutifully went out onto the balcony, from where he neither saw nor heard anything untoward.

When he returned Jamie had already poured him a drink which was waiting for him on the small table between the two comfortable chairs. Mortimer took a sip and looked questioningly up at Jamie. "Is it just Scotch and water?"

"Damn," said Jamie, "I think I must have put soda in by mistake. Sorry."

"Don't worry," said Mortimer, "it makes quite a pleasant change."

"Good health, Mortimer."

Mortimer raised his glass. "Yours too, Jamie."

CHAPTER 18

When Mortimer awoke what seemed like two or three days later, thick-headed and sluggish, Jamie was standing at his bedside looking anxious.

"You all right, old man?"

"Whatever happened?"

"We got rather stocious, I'm afraid. Ramon had to replenish the mini-bar."

"But –"

Before Mortimer could say any more there was what sounded like a deafening blast from the ship's tannoy: "Will all passengers please go immediately to their staterooms and remain there until further notice. There was a most regrettable incident on the upper deck last night and four men were lost overboard. They are now presumed to be drowned and foul play is suspected. Will all passengers remain in their staterooms until they have been cleared by security. We regret …"

Jamie turned the tannoy switch down.

"But I hardly had a drink, Jamie. Not much at dinner and you only poured me a scotch when I got back but after that –"

There was a knock at the door and two burly black security men came in without waiting for a reply.

"Good morning," said one and turned to his assistant. "Lock the door and the balcony window, Morgan. You may get out of bed, Mr Trippe." It was without doubt an order rather than a request. "And stand next to Mr Munro." He nodded to the unspeaking Morgan, who efficiently frisked both the suspects. "Good. Now sit down. Both of you."

Mortimer soon realized that he and Jamie were in considerable trouble, or one of them was. It seemed that the 'incident' had taken place shortly after midnight when two passengers had heard shouts from the top deck and what sounded like a scuffle followed by four splashes. The incident had not actually been witnessed, but both the passengers had noticed a man on his own climbing the steps towards the top deck where four other men had apparently been enjoying a late evening stroll, albeit that it was drizzling. These other men concerned had all apparently been Londoners and quite distinctive in appearance: two were tall and angular, two short and stocky; three had fashionably shaven heads whilst one, although white, had dreadlocks; each wore a different coloured dinner jacket; in short, they were all – or had been – unmistakeable. The solitary man seen mounting the steps had worn an unusual black straw hat and carried a black cane, or what looked like a black cane. Security were well aware that Trippe and Munro made a regular habit of going for a bedtime walk on the upper deck and that Trippe invariably carried this black stick and in poor weather wore a black straw hat instead of his usual Panama. In view of the foregoing it must be obvious that Trippe was the prime suspect, but it could not be ruled out at this stage that Munro had been some sort of accomplice.

"But this is ridiculous," said Mortimer, a little unconvincingly. "I didn't even go out on deck last night."

The chief security man ignored him and turned to Jamie.

"Me neither," replied the Scot.

The security man looked back at Mortimer. "So you deny the obvious?"

"Of course I deny it," Mortimer said hotly. "Anyway how could I have done what you say with that cane? It would have been four to one, remember, and the Sink Street Mob are all professional East End thugs."

"You admit knowing them, then?" He paused significantly. "And you don't deny being armed with an offensive weapon, do you?"

"That?" said Mortimer, pointing at his cane, which stood in its usual place. "Why, you could hardly harm a mouse with it, let alone four hardened gangsters."

The security man picked up the cane and examined it minutely. "I take your point, Mr Trippe, that *on the face of it*, it is not the obvious choice of weapon for a killer."

"There you are," said Jamie exultantly, "you're in the clear, Mortimer."

But Mortimer, no believer in tempting fate, was not so hasty. The security man, still holding the black cane, pressed an almost invisible button just below the silver knob. To Mortimer's astonishment, there was a click and a few inches of gleaming steel became visible between the knob and the black stem of the stick. With obvious satisfaction the security man withdrew a long, narrow sword, and pointedly felt with his finger its razor-sharp edge. It was a swordstick! And Mortimer had never known. He realized that there must have been more to dear old Grandfather Trippe than met the eye. But that was no help now, and it would clearly be useless to deny that he had known that the wretched cane contained a sword. He remained silent.

"So?" said the security man. Still Mortimer said nothing.

But now Jamie spoke up. "Wait a minute," he said.

"I didn't ask you," snarled the security man.

"I don't care whether you asked me or not, you blasted bully," Jamie said stoutly. "You just damn well listen for a change."

Clearly not accustomed to bring thus addressed, it was the security man's turn to remain silent.

"Mr Trippe couldn't possibly have done what you say, for the simple reason that he was here, in bed, drugged to the eyeballs."

"Drugged? Do you take drugs, Mr Trippe? the chief security man accusingly asked, but received in reply only a blank stare.

"He doesn't like to admit it," continued Jamie, "but he's a poor sleeper and I think he rather overdid it on the sleeping pills last night. I never use them myself so I don't know what's a normal dose, but I remember I was quite worried at the time. The bottle, or what's left of it, is in that bedside table."

"Just check that, Morgan." Morgan did, and found an almost empty bottle.

"An empty bottle of sleeping pills hardly constitutes an alibi," said the security man, but now with markedly less confidence.

"There's a ship's doctor on board," said Jamie. "If you don't believe me, it's easily checked with him."

The security man picked up the telephone.

By the time that the grizzled and no-nonsense doctor had examined Mortimer and expressed the firm opinion that he must have been virtually comatose for at least ten hours, and probably nearer twelve, and was in fact lucky to be alive, it began to look as though the security man's case against the detective – whatever he might have thought privately – must have completely collapsed. There being no other suspects, he would surely be obliged to discontinue this line of enquiry and the deaths would have to be presumed to have been either accidental or, more likely, caused by a fight between the victims themselves. And so it was but no one was able to account for the presence near the scene of the man in the black straw hat carrying the black cane.

As the two security men left, Jamie mopped his brow in relief and said, "Phew, that was a close thing."

"I was very grateful to you, Jamie. But what on earth did happen?"

"It's a bit of a long story," said Jamie. "Let's have a drink, even if it is a bit early, and I'll tell you." He opened two quarter bottles of champagne and poured them one each. "Briefly," he said, "the hulk Cyril, at the behest of the Sisters, of course, in effect asked me to assist in bumping you off."

"What!?"

"I'd better explain."

The Sisters, Jamie said, had found out that Mortimer was up to something which was likely to do them no good – though he'd no idea what – and wanted him 'out of the way'. Cyril was their link with the baddies and they'd asked him to get the Sink Street wallahs to do the necessary. For a fee, of course. They knew that he and Mortimer usually went for a midnight walk and thought that this would be the best time for some sort of action, although not necessarily murder. But Mortimer would have to be alone, as the Sisters knew from Cyril that Jamie was quite useful in a scrap. So Jamie had decided to take Mortimer's place, black hat and cane and all. He'd considered telling Mortimer first but thought he might object: hence the sleeping pills which he'd obtained from the ship's dispensary; Jamie apologized if Mortimer was still feeling a bit groggy, but all was well that ended well, so to speak.

"But what did you do up on deck?"

"Well, when these characters came for me I took the hat off – didn't want to lose it overboard or anything – and the moment the blighters recognized me they scarpered. I think a couple of them may have jumped overboard to get away." He paused. "In fact they may all have done, I'm not sure. Some may even have made it to the shore, for all I know. Anyway we're not likely to be troubled by them again."

Mortimer looked doubtful. "And didn't it occur to you that you must have been Suspect Number 2? You were the only other person with access to the hat and the cane, you know."

"I allowed for that," said Jamie. "I told fat Cyril that I'd need an alibi. Preferably a woman who'd swear that I'd been with her all night, if necessary. As it turned out, it wasn't needed. The security blokes must be pretty dim not to have thought of it. But I suppose that's about par for the course."

"Maybe they were just intimidated by your manner," said Mortimer. "But did you find your woman?"

"Oh yes, that was easily arranged. The Frog Sister Louise apparently hasn't been pulling her weight much Sister-wise and this was something she could do for them, so she volunteered. Bound to be believed too, being French and not a bad-looker. As an added precaution I had a cup of tea with her before breakfast this morning so her stateroom chap would see me and back up her story. Nice touch that, I thought."

Mortimer wasn't sure how much of Jamie's story was to be believed; some of it did rather stretch credulity but whatever the details, that the man had saved his life could not be doubted. "I can't thank you enough, Jamie," he said.

"Think nothing of it, my dear fellow. We're pals, aren't we? Incidentally lunch in Tallinn tomorrow's on me. I was paid quite well. Fifty per cent down and fifty per cent on completion. They can't take the first half back, whatever they might think of the outcome." Jamie grinned and took another sip of champagne.

* * *

By the time that the Lucky Lady was safely docked in Tallinn Jamie's mood of listlessness and gloom, so noticeable over the past days, had been completely transformed, displaced Mortimer could not help suspecting, by whatever events had taken place on the upper deck two nights before; he was now on the peak of his form, cheerful and optimistic almost to the point of euphoria. For his lunch treat he had dressed in a freshly pressed white silk suit matched by a pale blue silk shirt (which Ramon said had somehow got 'mixed up' in the laundry, replacing a frayed old cotton garment of Jamie's whose only resemblance had been its colour) and a Brigade of Guards tie. Any aspirations which Mortimer might have had to equal this near-perfection fell well short, but with a dark blue blazer, white duck trousers and his Panama hat, his appearance certainly proclaimed his nationality if not the excellence of his tailor, as they set off for the Estonian capital in high spirits.

Mortimer, although remaining constantly on the *qui quive*, still believed that the kidnap attempt would not take place until Helsinki. He was, therefore, more than a little disconcerted as they descended the gangplank to see, not far ahead of them on the quay the five Chameleons, all got up in what he imagined was traditional Estonian costume. Was this to be their cover for their real role as kidnappers, he wondered as it suddenly also struck him that this was the first time that he had seen the musicians ashore. Furthermore, not far in front of them, were Mr Nkoto and his wife and it seemed to Mortimer as though the folklorish-looking Estonians were following *them*. Mortimer still had no plan as to how to prevent or abort the kidnap and his mood of elation was thus swiftly dampened. But not for long. For after they had passed through customs he beheld a sight which was a joy to any man's eyes: Cissie, with her rudimentary disguise now removed looked like the proverbial million dollars in a figure-hugging scarlet dress and her black hair and eyes sparkling like diamonds. Mortimer could see that the effect of this apparition had clearly hit Jamie like a hammer, whilst his own mind was further lightened by Bert's appearance of obvious vexation, which was not mitigated by the fact that he had troubled neither to shave nor to put on any even tolerable clothes. Jamie invited the couple to join him and Mortimer for a 'celebratory' lunch before Mortimer had the chance to utter the barest greeting and Cissie, presumably at the prospect of having the company of her 'husband' at least diluted for a time, had joyfully agreed, whilst Bert, although manifestly not pleased at the suggestion, grudgingly accepted. By this time Mortimer was becoming anxious that he might lose sight of the Chameleons and their quarry and urged the others not to shilly-shally in following him into the town. At one of the most abundant and colourful flower-stalls that Mortimer had ever seen, on the edge of town, Jamie stopped to buy Cissie an armful of the finest blooms, quixotically waving away the change from a large denomination note and presenting his purchase with a bow to the ecstatic Cissie. Again Mortimer strained his eyes for the Chameleons and hurried on. It was not long, however, before two of them disappeared into a liquor store and came out only moments later with several bottles; soon after this, they all vanished into some sort of dive bar from which, to judge by the loud music and singing even at that time of day, it seemed unlikely that they would emerge in time or in the frame of mind to kidnap anyone. It was still too early to look for a restaurant for lunch so Mortimer decided that they should do their sight-seeing in the wake of the United Nations man and his wife, who were suitably armed with maps and guide-books and generally seemed to be taking the pleasures of their visit as seriously, Mortimer thought, as befits a man who may have little time left for such entertainment. Jamie and Cissie, now deeply engrossed in conversation with each other, followed obediently and unseeingly, while Bert was too grumpy even to complain at the unwonted exertion. Fortunately for Mortimer Mr Nkoto seemed to be no more of an enthusiast for museums than he himself was but possibly drawn by its marked difference from the prevailing baroque of Tallinn's Lutheran churches dragged his wife enthusiastically into the Russian Orthodox cathedral of Alexander Nevsky, whither Mortimer and his party, dutifully in one case and automatically in the others, followed. When they eventually came out Jamie was clearly prepared to put off his lunch treat no longer.

"Time to look for a decent restaurant," he said, and they headed for Town Hall Square. To Mortimer's relief, Mr and Mrs Nkoto had clearly arrived at the same decision and disappeared into a restaurant advertising 'genuyne Estonian kweezeen'. It was not until, not far away, Jamie had found a restaurant called Gloria, which claimed to be the oldest and most prestigious in town and a haunt for the rich and famous, that he appeared satisfied. Certainly the menu displayed outside more than supported the assertion that it was for the rich. As Jamie went inside he suggested politely to Bert that he might like to bring up the rear 'so as not to give a false impression.' Bert glowered but complied.

Once inside it was immediately made clear that they could not be served without a reservation having been made but Jamie said that that was perfectly all right; they would take a bottle of the finest French champagne available while they waited, and could another bottle please be put on ice for their convenience in due course? It was not long before they were seated at a window table, with waiters fussing round in an embarrassingly sycophantic manner. To Mortimer's astonishment, Jamie ordered food which, combined with the champagne, the detective guessed would probably account for a considerable portion of the Sisterhood's advance payment to him. As they were waiting for the first course, Elspeth Sturdy unexpectedly appeared from the street and strode magisterially through the door but was sharply pulled back by the tails of her jacket when the other Sisters had taken one glance at the menu outside. Gloria, annoyed at being baulked in her intention of having lunch in the restaurant which bore her name, remained looking yearningly through the window. Until, that was, she saw Jamie, who was mouthing words which she seemed to understand as well as making nasty faces at her.

"That'll teach 'em to try to bump you off, Mortimer," Jamie said and Bert looked at him with dimly dawning half-understanding, and did not speak for the rest of the meal. Jamie and Cissie flirted outrageously and Jamie order a third bottle of champagne.

When they returned to the Lucky Lady Cissie had to be physically supported by her 'husband', who had now very much recovered the power of speech – even if it was largely confined to some of the less polite expressions of the English language – and they all received some curious and knowing looks from the ship's security people. Mortimer thought that it had been an excellent day.

CHAPTER 19

By the time that Mortimer went down for his smoked salmon the following morning the Lucky Lady was already docking in Russia's largest sea port. To avoid the nuisance of visas and other bureaucratic irritations Mortimer had, at considerable expense to his client, booked a guided tour of St Petersburg in what was described as a limousine. As this seemed rather extravagant for one person he had suggested that Jamie should join him, free of charge of course; this offer had been gladly accepted for the Scot, unlikely as it seemed, appeared to have an almost pathological fear of being left on his own for long periods. Mortimer suspected that this may have been due to the 'charming rogue' being accustomed to the company of women, although until recently he had had no luck in that direction on this trip. Mortimer was looking forward to the trip round St Petersburg and he had brought his travel guide with him to the breakfast table since Jamie always seemed to be the first to pounce on any guide 'bumf' available in the stateroom. For some quite unaccountable reason the former tour guide was quite unable to find St Petersburg in his book. He was still looking for it when he was joined by Jamie, who this morning had given his session in the gym a miss in order to be on time for Mortimer's guided tour.

"I don't seem to be able to find St Petersburg in this damn thing. It's not under either 'S' or 'P'."

Jamie picked up the fat red book and read aloud: "'Nagle's USSR Travel Guide'." He turned over two or three pages. "'Copyright 1966 by Nagel Publishers, Geneva (Switzerland).' What do you expect?"

"Oh, er, I see. Leningrad back in those days, I suppose."

On the quay they met Bert and Cissie, once more wearing her ridiculous shawl and peasant dress, but clearly relieved to be off the ship. As they obviously had no visas, without which it seemed impossible to do anything unless you had arranged a guided tour, Mortimer suggested that they too should also join him in the limousine, although he was a little sheepish about admitting that he had hired one. It seemed a reasonable enough offer, however, since Bert – well, Lady Bertha – was after all picking up the bill. The offer was again accepted, but this time with a wry smile from Bert. Mortimer soon found a young woman standing beside a vast limousine and holding in her hand a cardboard placard which bore the legend in large capital letters: TRIPE. By this time Cissie had somehow contrived to disrobe. After brief negotiations with Anna, for such was the overbearing young Russian lady's name, during which a hundred-dollar bill changed hands, they all climbed in and were soon on their way. Whether because of inadequate English or sheer pig-headedness none of Anna's passengers ever found out, but she ignored all instructions and requests and went her own sweet way, uttering the while a non-stop and only partly intelligible commentary, presumably giving details of the vast number of 18th and 19th century neo-classical buildings – which to Mortimer all looked to be in similar colours and in the almost empty streets to be from some gigantic stage-set – and across the almost equally large number of bridges which criss-crossed the city. It seemed impossible that so few of the city's five million inhabitants should be at large in its ample squares, parks, boulevards and broad streets. Although it was a lovely sunny day, the place seemed like a ghost town and Anna's heavily accented and robotic monologue did nothing to redress this spooky impression. Mortimer did work out, however, that they had seen – or should have seen on their impervious glide down numerous unpronounceable 'prospekts' – the Peter and Paul Fortress and Cathedral, the Winter Palace, the Nevsky Prospect, the Summer Garden and most memorable of all, St Isaac's Cathedral, apparently St Petersburg's largest church.

Outside the latter edifice, Anna showed for the first time some genuine enthusiasm when she saw an enormously long white stretch-limousine and announced that the presence of this somewhat unexpected conveyance betokened the solemnization within of an 'upper-class' marriage. The wedding was, of course, conducted according to the rites of the Russian Orthodox Church and the booming opera-trained voice of the heavily bearded priest was accompanied by all the trappings and rituals to be expected from such an occasion. What seemed strangest to the visitors, however, was not the actual wedding ceremony but that simultaneously in the same building there were also taking place not only a christening, which Mortimer thought might be vaguely appropriate, even if it did draw attention to the waistline of the white-robed bride, but also a funeral, which he felt to be markedly less appropriate.

When they were once more outside, Mortimer thought that he had succeeded in persuading the mulish Anna that they wished to go first to a typical Russian bar, where they might see some normal townspeople, and secondly to a cheapish restaurant, the sort where local people could be expected to have a weekday lunch, and there to eat something typical along the lines of Borscht followed perhaps by Stroganoff. Anna, albeit with a dismissive shrug, appeared to agree to these two simple requests. Bert only wished that Lady Bertha had been present to see off this impudent young female, for he knew that he himself had no more chance with her than had Mortimer.

The 'bar' turned out to be a souvenir shop in which the party from the Lucky Lady were the only customers. Here they were blackmailed by the offer of a free cup of coffee and a cheap vodka into each buying some sort of token and Mortimer, for the exorbitant price of 10 dollars, ended up with a keyring depicting on one side the Winter Palace and on the other a particularly thuggish looking portrait of Vladimir Putin. For lunch Anna proudly showed them into a very expensive and obviously far from typical restaurant. Wallpaper, tablecloths and napkins were all of bright yellow and the customers, except for an English-speaking party in the middle of the room, all apparently drawn from what under Communist rule had been called the *nomenklatura*, and even now by the look of them of the same ilk – favoured state employees of one sort or another. The only bright point was the English-speaking party, also from the Lucky Lady, and whose guide Anna greeted cordially. Again from his experience with Eurolux Tours, Mortimer guessed that the two Russian guides' motive for bringing their charges here was a meal to their taste with excellent wine and a commission commensurate with the extortionate prices. The food certainly was not to Mortimer's taste: it was a most unpleasant Russian version of *nouvelle cuisine*, which he found almost inedible, although the horrible Anna not at all surprisingly, clearly loved every morsel.

The light relief from the people in the English speakers was provided mostly by the black Harvard law professor, who did not appear to be anything like a law professor, or any sort of professor at all or even a university man if it came to that. He never smiled, but grinned and laughed a great deal, mostly at his own remarks, and had more the appearance and general demeanour of a jazzman from New Orleans than that of a Bostonian lawyer. At the approach of a tight-skirted and full-bottomed waitress he administered with one of his enormous hands a cordial slap of greeting to her rump and laughed prodigiously.

"Don't worry, my dear," the Harvard man's wife told the young waitress, "he does that to everybody."

"He must be a busy man," said the Russian girl tolerantly and continued imperviously with her duties.

There were six of them at the table, two other Americans, who hardly uttered a word between them, and an English couple. They had clearly just met for the Englishman now said: "I think we should introduce ourselves. My name is James Sparrow, and this is my wife Elspeth."

"Glad to know you, James," said the Professor. "Elspeth," he added with a faint bow. "I'm Hal P. Hobday Junior – sometimes known as Armstrong – and this is my wife Betty. These are our friends." He waved vaguely in the direction of the other American couple and mumbled something which might or might not have been an introduction. "Now you're probably wondering what my initial 'P' stands for. You Britishers always do. Well, I'll tell you. It stands for 'P'. Nothing more, nothing less. Not Peter, not Paul, not Percival as it might in your country, just for simple ole 'P'. What would I want with another name? Hal's good enough for me and it was good enough for my father and his father before him. The 'P's been passed down in the family for generations. It came from a slave owner when we were in servitude in the South, and it was good enough for him too. That satisfy you?"

"I never asked," said Mr Sparrow.

"You were just going to. I could hear it on the tip of your tongue. Anyway enough of me."

There was a lull for about three seconds, which the professor presumably considered it impolite not to fill, and he continued. "My profession is the law. I have risen to the rather tedious position of Professor of Law at Harvard University, of which establishment you will have heard. My speciality is intellectual property rights. When I was at the bar in Boston I was the only practitioner with any knowledge of the law of copyright relating to jazz music, for which, or course, it is necessary to know about jazz, which, of course, I do. I should have stuck to that. Matter of fact," and here he looked round the room carefully to ensure that he was overheard, "I shall probably soon be going back to it," he said, if anything raising his voice. At this point Bert took the opportunity to pluck Mortimer on the sleeve. "Mortimer," he said, "I think it's time we had a chat."

"Not now, please, Bert. I'm listening to the professor. This may be important."

"Important!" This confirmed Bert's fears that his hired sleuth was at best an incompetent investigator and at worst had – well, what would these days be called serious learning difficulties.

Betty glared at her husband. "You never told me this, Hal. What the Dickens do you mean?"

"Only heard this morning, dear. I've yet to accept, of course, but it may be so long Massachusetts and hi California."

"Well, you might have told me."

"Sorry, dear. Needed Dutch courage," said the professor improbably, refilling his glass from a bottle of Stolichnaya which had considerately been left on the table and downing it in one. It seemed to Mortimer that the apparently soon to be ex-Harvard professor had been more in need of an audience than of Dutch courage. "Anyway," continued the unrepentant professor, "the offer is of a partnership with the best law firm in Santa Monica, not far from Hollywood, which specializes in musical copyright. Jazz in my case. I should have stuck to jazz in the first place."

"Are you related to Louis Armstrong, by any chance?" Mr Sparrow asked politely, no doubt sensing that Hal's monologue would continue whatever he said.

"Funny you should ask that," said Hal. "The answer to your question, sir, is that I might be and I might not be. It is hard to say. There is no definite proof that I am, but on the other hand there is no definite proof that I am not. What matters is that I *feel* as if I am related to the great Satchmo. You understand?"

Mr Sparrow nodded and Betty suppressed a yawn. But then in a far corner of the restaurant, on a small dais and half-hidden behind a curtain, Hal Hobday-Armstrong spotted a yellow baby-grand piano. Before he could be stopped by staff or customers he was on his feet and at the keyboard. Standing in a crouching posture, for the piano stool was nowhere to be seen, he launched into a succession of Satchmo favourites. At the end of his performance he bowed deeply to unrestrained applause, even from the *nomenklatura*. "Do you know," he said, as he resumed his seat and picked up his glass, "I could play that stuff anywhere, literally anywhere, and on any instrument."

"Even on a church organ?" called out Mortimer unexpectedly.

"A church organ? Why, sir, I'd like nothing better than to play my namesake on a church organ. Thank you for your kind enquiry." He raised his glass to Mortimer, who responded in kind.

"Now, Bert," said Mortimer. "What was it that you wanted to discuss?"

* * *

Since the Lucky Lady was not due to leave St Petersburg until the following evening, it was still moored in the docks but Mortimer decided that this was no reason for him and Jamie to forgo their bedtime deck walk, although this normally took place while they were at sea. Usually during their walk on the top deck it was seldom that they saw anyone else but tonight, no doubt because they were in port, quite a number of people were taking the air. As usual Mortimer carried his cane and wore his Panama hat, which he doffed to the few people with whom he was on nodding acquaintance. Jamie was not merely unsociable but obviously nervous, even twitchy as well, and his eyes constantly searched the dim light for Mortimer could not guess what. Suddenly a man's voice greeted them from behind.

"Good evening, gentlemen."

Jamie spun round and Mortimer glanced over his shoulder. It was Major Fox-Vasey, the long-suffering husband of the appalling Ursula Fox-Vasey, who had recognized Mortimer from his Eurolux tour.

"Good evening, Major," said Mortimer. "All alone?"

"My wife has taken to her bed, thank God," replied the Major, adding hastily, "thank God, I mean, that it is nothing serious."

"I quite understand," said Mortimer sympathetically. "Has she seen the doctor?"

"No, no, nothing like that. Just something she ate in St Petersburg, I think, Mr Trippe."

"What did you have?"

"Borscht and Stroganoff."

"Well lucky you," said Mortimer.

The Major gave Mortimer an odd look. "It certainly has its silver lining, I grant. Anyway, nice to see you." And Major Fox-Vasey strode into the gloom.

Jamie had kept uncharacteristically quiet during lunch, no doubt mostly on account of the professor's extraordinary garrulity. Indeed neither he nor Cissie had spoken much at all during the whole visit to St Petersburg, probably, Mortimer thought, because it had been far from conducive to flirtation. Now, however, Jamie suddenly turned to Mortimer.

"Why were you so interested in that awful professor, Mortimer?"

"Oh, it was just a thought I had. Probably won't come to anything, though."

CHAPTER 20

Since they had one more day in St Petersburg Mortimer, having, he thanked God, not booked another personal guided tour and having no visa, was obliged to stay on board. This suited him well for he had a great deal to think about and another visit to Blossom at her little bar beside the swimming-pool would suit his purpose admirably. Including, of course, a hamburger. They would sail for Helsinki that evening and be there early the next morning, so there was no time to be lost. The fact that, unlike at the other ports except St Petersburg, they were to have two full days in the Finnish capital, which would give the Chameleons time both to establish whatever contacts they must have made there and to carry out their deed, even if they did not have the chance to return to the ship before it left, seemed to confirm what was now a firm conviction in Mortimer's mind: that this was to be where the kidnap would take place. Obviously it was now too late for Tallinn, and that, apart from Helsinki, only left Stockholm, which he excluded for a number of reasons: the Chameleons would have no common language; it was too heavily built up and densely populated and far less remote; and its offshore islands were all summer holiday retreats whose cabins and villas would at this time of year be mostly occupied and busy not just with holidaymakers but with small seaborne craft of one sort or another. It had to be Helsinki, and they were nearly there. The talkative, jazz-playing Harvard professor at lunch the previous day had inadvertently supplied Mortimer with what he thought was rather a good idea, if only he could devise some realistic means of putting it into effect. But at present he could not, and did not seem likely to. The situation was becoming desperate.

Mortimer had at last decided that, after all his doubts, he trusted Jamie more or less implicitly. The man was moody and impulsive certainly, probably dishonest in a relatively innocent sort of way and also, it now turned out, not above a bit of what he called 'rough stuff' when it was necessary. But Mortimer had concluded that Jamie was essentially a decent man and he could not have wished for a more loyal friend. The Scot was also in touch with the criminal fringes of this imperfect world and obviously knew about some of the more undesirable elements on the Lucky Lady. The detective badly needed some support, and Bert was clearly worse than useless, so Mortimer had decided with some reluctance to confide in Jamie; it would be better if something went wrong in an attempt than merely to sit back and wait for the inevitable. Jamie had been delighted to accept Mortimer's suggestion that he should join him for a drink or two and a hamburger ('can be damn good, but can be quite foul' was Jamie's verdict on the dish), and here they were now *chez* Blossom, who without being asked, brought them both a beer. The Scot was at first distracted by a lightly tanned young blonde climbing out of the pool, but soon lost interest.

"I've been thinking," he said eventually.

"So have I," replied Mortimer.

"As a matter of fact," continued Jamie, "I could do with your help on a rather delicate matter."

"And I with yours, Jamie."

Jamie laughed. "Mutual back-scratching, eth? Shall I kick off first?"

"Please do."

Jamie explained that his problem mostly concerned 'the hulk Cyril'. He had already told Mortimer, he said, that the Sisters used Cyril for all the dodgy stuff and this of course had included what was supposed to have happened on the upper deck that evening. Well as a result of that Cyril was more than somewhat in the Sisterhood's bad books and Jamie had thought that he himself would also be a trifle out of favour with Cyril, but this had turned out not to be the case. The big man apparently in fact rather sympathised with him now, as he understood what good pals he and Mortimer must be; he could do with a pal himself, he'd said, but he'd never really ever had one. Also he'd never liked those Sink Street bastards, so good riddance was his verdict and well done, Jamie, whatever he *had* done. Anyway the bloody Sisters were now treating him like pure shit, as if it hadn't been bad enough before. They'd threatened to shop him to the Met back in London, even for things *they'd* ordered him to do, if he didn't do exactly as he was told; and it would be the words of four respectable women against one man, who was already known to the police. In future not only would his wages be halved but any pretence of equality completely out of the window. He would be nothing better than a fucking slave. So what did Mortimer think that Cyril now wanted?

"Revenge?" suggested Mortimer.

"With knobs on, old man. And I can't think of a blessed thing to suggest."

"I can," said Mortimer without hesitating. "I can think of just the thing."

And now Mortimer did the explaining. What would hurt the Sisters more than anything, he said, would be for their plans to fail completely.

"What plans, old man?"

Mortimer had forgotten that Jamie knew nothing of the intended kidnap attempt, or of how the Sisters were behind it, still less of his own involvement. He decided to tell all, including the two conclusions he had so far reached and how he had reached them, and his plan to abort the whole thing with the unwitting help of the Harvard man, which he had until now been unable to think of any way of implementing.

"But you've just given me an idea, Jamie." Even as he spoke Blossom approached with an already uncorked bottle of red wine and two wine glasses and placed them on the table.

"That look good, gentlemen?"

"Spot on," said Mortimer.

"Just the ticket," said Jamie, draining his beer and gratefully allowing Blossom to pour the wine. He looked at Mortimer. "Anyway what's this idea?"

"Well, one way of giving the Sisters a nasty poke in the eye would be to make them kidnap the wrong man. Agreed?"

"Good God! Anyway, agreed."

"So that, with Cyril's help, is what we do."

"But how?"

Mortimer then reminded Jamie of the Harvard professor's conversation and behaviour in the St Petersburg restaurant at lunchtime the previous day: of his apparent imperviousness to everything except what he himself was saying at any given moment; of the fact that he didn't seem to give a damn about Harvard and would anyway soon be leaving; and of the fact that Mortimer had coaxed from him his great desire to play jazz on a church organ.

"Forgive me if I'm being dim," said Jamie, "but I don't quite follow your drift."

"He also happens to bear some resemblance, though admittedly not a particularly close one, to the Secretary-General elect of the United Nations."

"Now I *am* lost."

"Well," said Mortimer, "we simply induce the Sisters' gang – these Chameleons, as I told you – to grab the Harvard man instead of the UN man." Mortimer said that what he proposed to do was to tell the jazz-playing Hal Hobday, that he, Mortimer, happened to know the organist at Uspenski Cathedral in Helsinki. This was the largest Orthodox church in Europe, as it happened, its interior a wondrous cavern of icons, crosses, altars and gleaming gold, which should be an ideal and novel venue for a short organ recital of the finest jazz from New Orleans. The church served Helsinki's large Russian population and Russians, as the professor would be well aware, were great jazz enthusiasts. Mortimer knew all this, he would explain to Hal, because the cathedral organist had formerly been an organ scholar at Keble College in Oxford, and was also a jazz lover, as Mortimer had found out when they had met as undergraduates at the Oxford University Jazz Club, nearly thirty years ago. He was sure that there would be no difficulty in arranging to have a short session on the organ, as Boris would probably still remember him. "How does that sound, Jamie?" Mortimer asked.

"I nearly believed it myself," answered the Scot, "but I still don't see where it gets us."

"Well, we know from our visit to Tallinn that Mr Nkoto, the UN man, is an avid visitor of Russian Orthodox cathedrals, so I also spin a yarn to him, with whom I've established some sort of nodding acquaintance, about the cathedral verger, and there we are," said Mortimer.

"You mean you get Nkoto talking to the verger by telling him that the chap would be happy to give Mr and Mrs N. a personal guided tour or something and then you get the Chameleons or whatever they call themselves to snatch the black chap talking to the organist and not the black chap yakking to the verger."

"That's it. Or rather, *you* get the Chameleons to do this, via the vengeful Cyril, who himself can easily make the excuse that the Chameleons simply got the two black men mixed up."

Jamie didn't even need a moment's thought to consider the idea. "Its brilliant," he said. "It can't go wrong."

"It could," said Mortimer, with typical caution. "Oh, and get Cyril to check the Chameleons' disguise is OK. They must have something in mind, but obviously we don't want these blighters walking into the cathedral wearing balaclavas and obviously armed to the teeth, do we?"

"I take your point, Mortimer."

"Good. OK?"

"Fine. OK so they snatch the wrong bloke, which nicely dishes the Sisters, avoids an international incident and all that, but what about poor old Hal?"

"You mean his own well-being might be compromised?"

"Well, wouldn't it?"

"I don't think so, Jamie. For a start he's got the hide of a rhino and is so egocentric that he's impervious to almost anything. His kidnappers won't achieve a thing. When they ring the telephone numbers in Harvard I'm going to give you, the Harvard people will laugh at them. They certainly won't cough up a cent. After all, the man's leaving them – they'll probably see it as desertion – and they've no longer any reason to pay a sausage for his release."

"But won't the kidnappers be so pissed off with friend Hal that they'll knock him off?"

"And risk a murder rap on top of anything else? Not a chance. They'll cut their losses, you can bet on that."

"I suppose you're right, Mortimer. But this all assumes that it will be Helsinki."

"It's bound to be. The only port after that is Stockholm, where the Chameleons will have no common language and no connexions. They're going to need guns, a getaway car, a boat, assuming they take our man to an island, and for all I know video and radio equipment and God knows what else as well. They'd probably guessed in advance that it would be Helsinki and quite likely made most of their arrangements in that dive bar we saw them disappear into in Tallinn. Somewhere, anyway, including disguise. Now it's over to you, Jamie."

Jamie raised his glance. "I confess I didn't think you had it in you, Mortimer."

"Most people don't, for some reason. I think that was probably why Mr Lamplighter took me on in the first place, it's a sort of cover."

* * *

Mortimer hadn't seen Bert all that day and it was only after dinner, which Mortimer suspected that he had been obliged to have with Cissie in their stateroom, that Lady Bertha's alter ego appeared in public. He looked far from well, hollow-eyed and visibly jumpy, and in the Piano Bar sat down uninvited at Mortimer and Jamie's table. He glanced nervously across at the Sisters who were as usual seated near the musicians and appeared to be in buoyant mood. Bert turned to Mortimer and, without any preliminaries, said that he hoped that all was in order for the next day.

"Everything shipshape, Bert," said Mortimer. "I can't say more than that."

Bert had no option other than to appear satisfied with this reply. They had not previously so much as mentioned the 'incident' on the top deck, but now Mortimer could resist the temptation no longer.

"Funny business, that cloak and dagger stuff the other evening, wasn't it? What did you make of it, Bert?"

Bert swallowed hard. "There was more to it than met the eye, if you ask me," he said guardedly.

"What puzzles me," Mortimer said innocently, "is what people like that were doing on a cruise in the first place. I image that someone must have hired them for some nefarious purpose."

"No reason why they shouldn't go on a cruise like anybody else," said Bert, "just because they look a bit spivvy."

"Good riddance, is what I say," muttered Jamie, beckoning the waiter.

At this moment Major Fox-Vasey, presumably on some sort of leave of absence from his wife and who was just passing, paused in his tracks.

"Good evening, gentlemen. Couldn't help hearing what you were talking about. Mind if I join you?" The Major clearly construed the ambivalent reaction of those seated as assent and pulled up a chair. "A bit rum, to put it mildly," he said. "I could have sworn I saw you going up those top steps, Mr Trippe, with your black hat and cane, but when I greeted you, you didn't reply."

"I didn't go up there at all that evening," said Mortimer, "as I explained to the security people."

"Funny about the hat and cane all the same," persisted the Major. Neither Mortimer nor Jamie said anything to this, but Bert gave them both a funny look.

CHAPTER 21

Mortimer had of course been obliged to ensure beforehand that the organist in the Uspenski cathedral (who had in fact never been closer to Oxford than London) would actually be there when the Harvard professor paid his visit. The detective had established from the Tourist Desk on board that an organ recital was to be given in the cathedral directly before evensong and that the recital was due to start at five o'clock. Mortimer decided, therefore, that it should be safe to arrive at about half past four and he assumed that the verger, or whatever his equivalent was in an Orthodox church, would be there pretty well all day, for in Mortimer's experience such men loved their churches so much that they willingly worked all hours for a pittance, often in physically less than comfortable circumstances. The detective gave instructions accordingly, to be passed down the line to Hal Hobday but himself made the necessary arrangements with Mr and Mrs Nkoto.

The Finnish capital greatly appealed to both Mortimer and Jamie, for it had an agreeable, light-aired, spacious and Northern character all of its own, with an immense boulevard, punctuated with colourful gardens and one small market, leading most of the way from where they disembarked to the very centre of the city. On Mortimer's map was shown something called the Esplanade and this boulevard certainly looked the part, unless the map was wrong – Mortimer found that a lot of maps appeared to be, but never were – which it was not. They found the local people not merely polite but genuinely good-humoured. In Senate Square they stopped for a beer and almost next to the bar where they had refreshed themselves they found a smallish restaurant for lunch, with an excellent view of the majestic if somewhat gaunt Lutheran cathedral that dominated the square from a small hill, reached from below by innumerable wide grey steps. The restaurant was exactly what they both wanted, and frequented by obvious office workers, no doubt of the better paid variety, which caused Jamie to remark mysteriously that it was 'just like being back at work'. After lunch they still had time to wander round the city centre before their tryst in the other, Orthodox cathedral.

They arrived at Uspenski Cathedral ten minutes before half past four and a few minutes later were joined by Mr and Mrs Nkoto, whom Mortimer quickly introduced to the verger-equivalent, to whom Mortimer had already briefly spoken about a possible tour of his beautiful church. Thankfully the professor had not brought his wife, no doubt because Mrs Hobday felt that there were more profitable things to do in Helsinki than listen to her husband play '*Ain't Misbehavin*' on the cathedral organ. Mortimer, avidly followed by a jazz-playing professor, and closely watched by Jamie, tapped the organist gently on the shoulder and the man turned to greet the visitors with gratifying enthusiasm. At this moment four tall monks and one short one, all dressed in flowing brown habits, materialized from under one of the intricately decorated arches, having been lurking, Mortimer could only suppose, behind two nearby black marble columns.

Mortimer saw Hal turn in surprise, but seemingly quite calmly. The organist uttered something sharply in what to Mortimer sounded like Russian while he himself suddenly heard a male hiss from the tallest monk, whom he could tell by the beaky nose was their leader. "Better take these two as well to be on the safe side," said the hiss in English, and the detective felt a non-too-gentle jab of something in the small of his back. He looked at Jamie, who whispered, "Not quite in the script, eh"

"Not exactly," muttered Mortimer, "but these things can happen, and in my experience often do."

Mortimer knew, and guessed that his Scottish friend also knew, that guns were not difficult to obtain in Finland, which he had read only recently in the papers had one of the highest rates of gun-ownership in the world, hunting being a favourite sport; consequently there was little doubt that the Chameleons' weapons were genuine. Mortimer had certainly never expected this. The biter bit, he thought ruefully. In a matter of moments the five monks and their three captives were outside and, without any great noise or fuss – shouting for help might only have been counter-productive – the three hostages were hustled into a waiting black minibus, its engine running and its immaculately uniformed driver clearly keen to be off. Scarcely a single member of the public had seen or heard a thing, and Mortimer thought that the whole operation had probably not looked particularly suspicious or even abnormal; the guns were invisible and the thing had been carried off smoothly and almost silently. In the back, Mortimer glanced at the former SAS man beside him but he merely smiled stoically and raised his eyebrows in resignation. They clearly had no chance.

As the minibus joined the heavy traffic to follow the harbourside road north towards the airport the general tension in the vehicle was mitigated only by the extraordinary composure of the main hostage himself. Always anxious to talk, and now with a captive audience, he began to describe some of the intricacies of musical copyright, particularly in its international aspects. Not knowing that the kidnappers were themselves musicians, the professor should not by right have had any reason to suppose that they would be interested in this somewhat specialized topic, but such considerations had never deterred Hal Hobday from expounding on any subject which interested him personally. He was, therefore, considerably gratified when the Beak began to ask him pertinent questions about certain details of his subject as they might be applied in particular to small musical groups who occasionally made recordings of their efforts, and on the relevance and enforceability of the various international treaties which might be applicable. This conversation was by no means exhausted when, to Mortimer's surprise, as he had expected their destination to be one of the islands well to the west of Helsinki, they turned sharply right, to the east, over a vast harbour bridge. Hal continued to drone on, apparently impervious to his predicament and seeming indeed to be hardly aware of what had taken place. Suddenly and without warning Mortimer found himself being handcuffed and blindfolded and realized that the same was happening to Jamie, though whether to Hal as well he could not tell. This he did not regard as entirely a bad sign since it indicated that the Chameleons must fear that the two of them might subsequently try to retrace their steps, probably with the police, and this in turn suggested that their lives would probably be spared. The Chameleons admittedly did not look like murderers, but Mortimer knew that this was by no means an infallible sign. Gradually the sound of the traffic grew less and eventually subsided to the point where there were obviously few other vehicles on the same road, although this left Mortimer no wiser; they could be travelling in any direction of the compass, but his guess was they really would now be heading west and that the first half hour, before the blindfolds were put on, had simply been an attempt to mislead. As Hal switched from topic to topic, increasingly losing the attention of his audience in the process, Mortimer realized that he had, if anything, underestimated the man's egocentricity and almost total lack of awareness of other people's reactions to anything.

After what Mortimer judged to have been about three hours in the minibus the driver suddenly brought it to a halt and the three prisoners were ordered out. Perhaps surprisingly, the blindfolds were removed and, although it was now nearly dark, Mortimer could see from the dim light ahead that the sun must have set over the sea in front of them which indicated, as he had supposed, that they had been travelling west. Their actual location, however, or anything approximating to it, remained a mystery. All that Mortimer could see clearly was the edge of a forest behind them and a motor launch moored on the shore in front with a boatman at the helm, who shouted a cheery greeting and was obviously expecting them. Beyond the launch in the fast darkening sea, were just visible numerous islands, although whether inhabited or not it was impossible to tell. Leaving the chauffeur with the vehicle, the Chameleons indicated with waves of their now clearly visible weapons that the captives should go aboard the launch and soon afterwards they were under way. For a merciful few minutes Hal had remained silent, but as the massive firmament above them began to disclose its sparkling treasures, hardly ever seen in London or anywhere else in or near a densely populated area, the wretched professor started another uninvited lecture. As a boy, he said, his ambition had for many years been to be a professional astronomer but although this, for reasons which he considerately said he would not bore them with, had never worked out he had put his knowledge of astronomy to good use when he had subsequently become a navigator in the US Air Force, even though to his chagrin he had never seen active service. The man clearly knew his subject and again began to hold the attention of the Chameleons to the point where Mortimer almost wondered whether his loquacious diversions were intended for some purpose other than the satisfaction of his own self-esteem. If nothing else, it seemed that the strange bond reputedly forged between kidnapper and hostage was in this instance forming with indecent speed. Mortimer knew, however, that any such bond would be of little use when the Chameleons discovered that their hostage could produce no ransom and was to that extent quite worthless; he also wondered with no little trepidation what effect this realization would have on his own and Jamie's fate. Even with occasional lights and log cabins, but no sign of human habitation, the numerous islands were for the most part featureless and almost indistinguishable. It was well over an hour before the helmsman cut the throttle and the launch glided silently into a rocky cove and drew alongside an obviously little used wooden jetty.

"Like a drink?" the Beak asked Hal once they were installed inside a comfortable looking but seemingly disused log cabin. The Beak and his accomplices still wore their monks' habits but were making no attempt to disguise their voices.

"Sure. What d'ya have?"

Mortimer and Jamie, both still manacled, were ignored and left in a corner as though quite forgotten.

"How about vodka with a beer chaser? Both local and not bad."

"Sounds good," said the American.

"Natalia, get that fire going, then we'll have some supper." The Beak glanced at Hal. "Have to be cold, I'm afraid." He glanced at his watch. "But we've got to make those phone calls soon, remember. Should be just about right with the time difference."

"Right" said the professor, raising one glass and then the other.

"What about our other guests?" said one of the monks. "They look harmless enough to me."

"OK," said the Beak, and the two unintended hostages had their handcuffs removed and were each given a beer but no vodka. "We don't want it running out," said the Beak. And Mortimer and Jamie were left in their corner, awaiting crumbs from the rich men's table.

While the others tucked into mountains of cold fish and meat, and various salads, all of which they washed down with by no means miserable quantities of red wine, the two envious onlookers had to make do with black bread and one more beer apiece. Once the meal was over the Beak pointed

201

to a telephone on a small table, clearly only very recently installed to replace the previous one, which now lay on the floor. "Right," he said to Hal. "You know why you're here."

" 'Course I know why I'm here. You want a fat ransom, right?"

"Right," said the Beak.

"And you'll get one, no problem," replied the hostage with considerable self-satisfaction. "I'm worth megabucks to those Harvard people, and don't you think I'm not. They're as rich a Croesus and just think of the shame if they didn't pay through the nose for the release of their second most eminent professor. Don't you worry, Mr Hostage Taker, they'll cough up millions for me. Just you see."

"Just as we thought," said the Beak, looking a little puzzled all the same, Mortimer presumed because he had never thought that the thing would be so easy, bonding or no bonding. "I have the list of telephone numbers here."

"Fine," said Hal. "You shouldn't need to go further than the top man, except of course that he'll need to confer with the main financial guy on the actual amount. What you looking for? Ten million into a Swiss bank account?

"More," said the Beak, obviously encouraged. "I had in mind double that."

"Good on you," said Hal. "But if you want my advice, don't push 'em above twenty."

"Not if you say so, Hal."

"I do say so. I guess they'll stick around twenty."

"Thanks for the tip." The Beak moved towards the telephone.

"Just a moment," said the Harvard man. "I've had a thought. Best if I talk with my secretary first. She's a good girl and knows me better than anyone. They might check with her. Make sure it's me and not some impostor. Also I want to cover my ass."

"Good thinking," said the Beak.

Hal nodded, picked up the telephone and dialled. He was through almost immediately. "Susie? It's me."

"Hal! Where are you?" Her voice was a clear as a bell to all in the cabin.

"I'm on vacation, as you know. Matter of fact, I've had to make a bit of a detour with some friends and they're going to be making a call to Schlumberger. We're having a great time and these guys – my hosts, you see, we're on some remote island – want to make sure it's OK for me to stay on for a bit. Better coming from them than me, see. Don't want anyone thinking I'm on the fast and loose or anything."

"I understand, Hal. What do you want me to say?"

"Tell Schlumberger everything's on the level, no funny business. And listen here, Susie. Listen carefully."

"Yes, Hal?"

"Whatever you do, not a word about Monica. They've no reason to suspect anything, but you know what Schlumberger is. Suspicion's his second name. I'll explain everything later. 'Bye." And he hung up.

"That done it, Hal?" asked the Beak.

"Sure. That's fixed it. Don't want them thinking I'm chasing skirt, that's all. Monica's a dame, see? No problem now. Over to you, and the best of luck." He waved a large hand at the telephone.

"Is that Mr Schlumberger?" asked the Beak when he got through; the deep male voice from America could also be clearly heard by all present in the cabin.

"You rang my number, didn't you. What d'you want?"

The Beak explained that he and some associates were holding Professor Hal Hobday at a destination which he was not at liberty to disclose, but the professor was in good health and Mr Schlumberger would have an opportunity to check this by speaking to him personally later if he so wished.

"Why would I want to speak with that bastard?" demanded Mr Schlumberger belligerently. "He doesn't interest me."

Obviously thinking that he had misheard, or at the very least that Schlumberger was bluffing, or possibly even trying to make a joke of the situation, the Beak began again, and this time was more explicit.

"I get it," said the voice down the line. "You want money for his release?"

The Beak looked at the other monks in obvious relief and once more spoke into the telephone. "That's it, Mr Schlumberger –"

"Well I'll give you money," said Schlumberger. "Don't say another word."

"But –"

"Where do you want it paid? You got an account in Switzerland?"

"In Zurich, yes."

"Name of bank and number of account?"

The Beak gave them over the telephone. "But we haven't discussed –"

"There's nothing to discuss, you jerk. Just keep Hobday exactly where he is, preferably on bread and water. For as long as possible. If I haven't heard from him in six weeks I'll pay five hundred bucks into your Swiss account for your trouble." And with this munificent offer Schlumberger hung up. The Beak turned furiously on his worthless hostage.

"Just what the fuck is going on?" he shouted.

Hal calmly explained about being offered a partnership with the law firm in Santa Monica and how he intended giving in his notice to the Harvard people through his secretary, later that day, as it happened. There must have been some confusion about the timing. As the monks might or might not know, it was several hours earlier in Santa Monica than in Harvard and that must have been the cause. It was a shame as he'd really wanted the monks to make a killing out of those Harvard bastards. Too late now, needless to say. Had they by any chance noticed the other black guy in the cathedral? The one who was also from the Lucky Lady and had been talking to the verger guy? Well, they should have snatched him instead, but it was too late now, dammit.

"Why him?" asked the Beak.

"Only that in a few weeks, he's going to be the new Secretary-General to the United Nations. Worth billions as a hostage. Get it?"

The Beak, who was far from being stupid, did get it. "Christ," he said.

"I'm surprised your employers didn't know that," said the Harvard man. "Must be pretty dumb."

"I'll tell them," said the Beak. "You're right, Hal. They sure as hell should have thought of that."

"Well guys," concluded the professor, "you can't say I didn't do my best."

"No man could have tried harder," agreed the Beak.

EPILOGUE

"And that's about it," said Mortimer. He was back in the smoking room of the Young Professionals' Club with Mr Lamplighter and the faithful Lionel, where both he and Lionel had once again unsuccessfully tried to decline Mr Lamplighter's well-intentioned offer of cherry brandy.

"Anyway you got back to the vessel in due time?" queried Mr Lamplighter.

"The next day we did, yes. After a pretty uncomfortable night in the log cabin. Hal made damn sure that we were there before the Lucky Lady sailed and he'd pretty well taken charge by that time. The rest of the cruise was comparatively uneventful."

"What an extraordinary business," said Mr Lamplighter. "And how did these Sisters as they call themselves react to the discovery that their wicked conspiracy had ignominiously failed?"

"Well, back on board the thing wasn't spoken about openly at all, even though there were whispers. Jamie told me that the Chameleons apparently pretended that they'd simply snatched the wrong black chap in the cathedral, which on the face of it sounds plausible enough. So Cyril Jinks got away with his little deception rather neatly. The Sisters were obviously furious all the same and after Helsinki took all their meals in Elspeth Sturdy's stateroom and never once showed their faces in public. The professor point-blank refused to say a word against his new-found friends the monks and in view of our part in the thing neither Jamie nor I was anxious to either, so nothing can really be proved. Anyway to implicate those behind the conspiracy would need Lady Bertha's backing, which she wouldn't give. The last thing she wants is any involvement with the law."

Mr Lamplighter then asked about 'the other matter'.

"Well, two bodies were eventually washed up on the Baltic coast somewhere near Tallinn but again there was no evidence to speak of and the Estonian authorities simply handed the thing over to the police in this country."

There had been an inquest in London, said Mortimer, but the coroner had directed the jury in view of the paucity of evidence and the highly unusual circumstances, to reach an open verdict; not, however, before he had permitted himself some well-chosen *obiter dicta* to the effect that a more positive outcome would almost certainly have been achieved if the security people on the Lucky Lady had conducted their enquiry with a little more assiduity. The upshot of the whole affair, concluded Mortimer, was that the police forces of three countries remained baffled by an apparent multiple murder at sea and what had looked to three or more honest and upright witnesses – including both the verger and the organist at Uspenski Cathedral – of a mysterious kidnapping by five cowled monks.

"I am delighted to hear it," said Mr Lamplighter, who regarded police detectives as state-controlled competition and held their methods largely in contempt. "More cherry brandy, gentlemen?"

"Not for me, thank you, Mr Lamplighter," said Mortimer who, without his host noticing, had 'accidentally' spilt his original one on the already well-stained carpet of the Young Professionals' Club's smoking room. The chief investigator looked now at Lionel.

"No thank you, sir. I find that more than one makes me sleepy."

"You are quite right, Lionel. You demonstrate admirable self-restraint. I shall on this occasion myself abstain for the same reason. I have to meet a new client after lunch." He turned back to Mortimer. "And Mr Scott-Munro?"

"He and Cissie Sykes are getting married. Tomorrow, as it happens."

"Married? Good Heavens above! Is this wise?"

"Probably not," said Mortimer. "But both are highly impulsive and there is no doubt that they are besotted with each other. It will be what Jamie described as his fourth time round the course and he has quite made up his mind that this will be the last. Cissie said that she was prepared to try anything once."

"God bless my soul!" exclaimed Mr Lamplighter, "I have to say that neither approach seems to me to betoken the state of matrimonial bliss contemplated by the marriage service ordained by the Book of Common Prayer."

"Then it is perhaps as well that they are to be married in Chelsea Register Office. And I wish them the best of luck," said Mortimer.

"As do I," said Mr Lamplighter, with little enthusiasm. He paused to take the last sip of his cherry brandy. "At all events," he said, "Lady Bertha appears to be more than satisfied. There was no trouble about the balance of the fees and she apparently did not query the very considerable expenses which were involved, including those necessarily incurred by my own participation. Am I not right, Lionel?"

"Quite right, sir." Lionel handed Mortimer a cheque. "That, Mr Trippe, is a little honorarium for Mr Scott-Munro, which Lady Bertha asked to be passed on to him. For his help in arranging the final result, you understand."

"Good Lord," said Mortimer. "She can't be aware of Jamie's – er, possible role in the demise of the Sink Street gentlemen."

"It would appear not," said Lionel.

Mortimer glanced at the cheque. It was for a thousand pounds. "I shall give it to him before the ceremony tomorrow. It will make a handsome wedding present."

"Incidentally, Mr Trippe," broke in Mr Lamplighter, "Lady Bertha asked me to pass on her personal thanks to you. She also said that the most satisfactory outcome had been achieved in spite of the somewhat unhelpful position adopted by Mr Bert Pyman, as I believe he was called. She now wishes to consign him to history."

"Consign him to history? What *can* she mean?"

"She has for some time been unhappy about the – er, duality of her identity and has now decided to regularize the matter once and for all."

Mortimer raised his eyebrows.

"By what used to be called, I believe, a visit to Casablanca," Mr Lamplighter announced with what struck Mortimer as unseemly glee. "Would that she had seen to that earlier," he added, not without considerable feeling.

"Speaking of clients," said Mortimer, "I cannot help feeling that I have been rather unlucky with my first two." Receiving no reaction from his superior, he continued. "The first, Mr Victor-Hugo St Pierre de St Briac on Malou turned out to be the fraudster whom I should have been pursuing in the first place, and even had the effrontery to have me wrongfully imprisoned. The second, the so-called Lady Bertha Hook, quite apart from anything else, tried to have me killed."

"Yes, yes, I know," Mr Lamplighter said quickly. "All most unfortunate. And you have risen above these difficulties, if I may say so, my dear Trippe, with consummate skill and ceaseless application to your duties. Lionel?"

"Mr Lamplighter has asked me to tell you, Mr Trippe, that your period of apprenticeship now being successfully completed, your monthly emolument is to be increased with immediate effect."

"Substantially, I believe," added Mr Lamplighter and, with unaccustomed embarrassment, rose to leave.

THE END